Upon the Pale Isle of Gloam

Written and edited by Mark Gulino

Cover design by Mark Gulino

Cover and interior art by Yornelys Zambrano Inojosa

Published by Mark Gulino

Book and Cover Design by Mark Gulino

Art and Illustrations by Yornelys Zambrano Inojosa

First edition, 2023

ISBN: 979-8-9892934-1-4

This story contains **mature content** and touches on topics some may be sensitive to. See the full **content warning** at the back of the book to learn more about it.

Dedicated to my wife, Stephanie.

I don't always believe in myself, but you
always believe in me. That's always enough.

Special thanks to: Mom and Dad, for supporting my endeavors—even when you aren't sure what I'm up to. Yornelys, who created the gorgeous artwork for the book cover. Ian, with whom I've always been able to share my passion for writing and storytelling. Aunt Sue, for showing me it's not impossible to pursue and achieve a dream. God, for giving me the inspiration for this story and the ability to write it.

Gray

The boat lay in silence upon the water. The black glass-like surface was stock-still and ominous, like a mirror in the dark, and reflected neither star nor moon nor sky. Not a sound could be heard in the night's infinite gloom, and it seemed as though existence itself had relinquished its ascendency leaving all but one ramshackle watercraft damned to drift in relentless suspension.

The woman opened her eyes to disquieting nothingness and wondered if she had drowned. She lay there in the boat, slipping in and out of consciousness, and when she was awake, she tried to remember things that did not permit her to, and while asleep, she dreamt of things she wished she had not. Soft voices whispered across the void. At first, they spoke comfort to her, but their words transmuted balefully to cachinnation in which horrific cruelty seethed. She dared not reply.

When the woman woke for the last time, many hours had passed. The sky above was a brooding gray. She sat upright and found that the vessel had wedged itself into the thick, wet sand of a shallow shoreline. Damp, frigid air clung to her cold, weary body. In despondency, she shivered and wept. Her tears were those of a girl who was broken and alone and deeply afraid.

The beach was littered with debris, both natural and man-made. There were boats and broken things and makeshift tents and lean-to's where others once made camp. The woman stood inside the watercraft and shifted her weight back and forth to balance herself. She lifted one leg over the side and then the other. Her wet shoes sank into the strand beneath them, which pulled and sucked at them with each step, and she trudged onward until the water could no longer reach her. Quivering, she surveyed the shoreline and scouted a small encampment where a fire pit had been artlessly cobbled together long before.

The woman remembered little of herself or her past, but her instincts remained unscathed. She gathered driftwood and cloth from the salvage and detritus and chanced upon a plastic lighter stripped of its label yet undepleted of its contents. When the woman gathered enough wood for a fire, she brought the materials to the pit and bundled twigs and leaves inside strips of torn cloth for kindling. She placed the driest logs over the kindling and set the damp ones along the edge to parch. She nursed the flames until they grew large enough that she no longer needed to tend them.

As the fire burned, so burned myriad questions. The woman was tired and hungry. She sat and stared into the dancing flames, and a single word surfaced from the farthest recess of her mind. *Rue*, she thought. *My name is Rue.*

As the day grew darker, Rue wandered the beach. She discovered an unopened can of yams in brown-sugar gravy and a sharp sliver of steel with which to open it. Burlap sacks, tattered and empty, were strewn about, and she collected those too. When Rue returned to the fire, she scraped out a space in the ground beneath a lean-to and filled it with the burlap and settled atop it with the canned yams. With three fingers, she spooned them to her mouth. Someone once told her that hunger was the best sauce, and though she could not remember who spoke these words, she could not agree more.

The blue-black veil of night draped itself over the shoreline. Rue rested beside the fire and fell asleep. She awoke in the darkness to a torturous wail piercing the brisk air. It came from the woods beyond the beach. Rue slid her arms across the ground, pushing waves of sand onto the fire to smother it. She feared what its glow might attract, for she knew not if this world was the same as that which she had once dwelled. She slept little that night.

The following morning, the sky was no less minacious and ashen than the evening prior, and thunder rolled overhead with an unwavering steadiness. Rue studied the shoreline with scrupulous sweeps of her eyes in hopes of finding a path toward civilization. She thought any way was better than traversing the forest but was overcome with dread when she saw no other way but through. Worse, the boat had been swept back into the sea while she slept.

Rue could not repel the crushing trepidation that filled her heart and mind much in the way that lungs draw air, so she decided she would stay at her camp until there was no other choice but to enter the forest that lay ahead. She made sweeping passes along the beach and rummaged through whatever she could find scattered throughout the dispersed piles of mangled watercraft. Shattered crates lay tangled in species of seaweed known only to faraway oceans. In her rummaging, she came upon a can of peaches in heavy syrup and several bars of granola. There was a large bag of peanuts and two batteries for a gadget that wasn't there.

When Rue returned to her camp, she ate the peaches and drank the syrup from the can and sucked the salt from the peanuts as she savored each one. Her hunger was satiated somewhat, but her thirst was unquenched. Looking at the sky and feeling a drop in temperature, she thought it might rain. She set out the empty cans from the food she had eaten and oscillated them into the coarse sand, hoping they would collect water.

In the evening, Rue still had no memory of her past or how she came to arrive at such a strange and foreboding place. She nestled into her improvised hollow beneath the lean-to and faded into sleep. A short time later, she opened her eyes and saw she was not alone. The paralyzing weight of terror flooded her veins, and she lay there, silent and unmoving.

Two figures loomed, silhouetted against the inky black of night. Their dull and lifeless eyes glowed white and were all but human. In whispering tones, they spoke to each other, and one said that Rue was quite beautiful and wished to lay with her; the other said it longed to pull the bones from her flesh while she agonied.

A distant crack of lightning ignited the horizon, and the beach was bathed in the luminous pale light. During the flash, the figures vanished, and when the light had gone, the figures remained. An unnatural weariness enveloped Rue. She could no longer keep awake. Despite her defiance, her eyes drew shut.

Rue fell into a fathomless sleep, drifting through dream after dream until dreams became nightmares. In one such nightmare, she found herself gazing upon the mouth of a cave, deeply nestled within a lush, narrow valley. A mother bear lazed there with her offspring.

The cubs played, giving little thought to the dangers of the surrounding world, for the sow was all the world they knew, and by some inherent instinct, they trusted that she would lay down her life to protect them. Rue observed them with a childlike curiosity. She admired the mother.

There came a rustling from a nearby patch of brush. A male bear reared up and let out an admonishing roar that echoed throughout the valley. Sensing its malice, the cubs cried out for their mother, but the sow did not move. She watched without so much as a twitch of a muscle or a sound of protest as the male lunged forward. It tore apart the screaming cubs. While blood and fur and flesh were flung in every direction, the sow stood silent, and Rue thought that a mother who would not protect her children was no mother at all.

It was the delicate pecking of raindrops upon Rue's face that woke her, and she jolted to her feet. She expected to see again the vile beings that appeared in the night, but they had gone. Rue checked her body with grave consternation. Deep scratches were etched into her calves and forearms. Dark bruises pressed upon her brown skin. She sobbed, knowing now that her fear of the isle was vindicated.

Rue worried she might be revisited and wished not to relive the encounter. On the beach was a broken section of metal hull that once belonged to a fishing boat. It was embedded within a low-lying dune. Its shell was enclosed but for one open side. Upon vetting the site, Rue thought she could fortify it, so she moved her camp inside and used planks of wood, incongruous and misshapen, to close the opening, save for a narrow passage she could crawl through. She sharpened the end of a long, blunt stick so that she could defend the entrance from invaders.

There was an uncluttered area of shoreline, and Rue thought it might make for an effective place to construct a signal. She had not seen nor heard any passing of aircraft but thought that should one fly overhead, a sign might garner the attention of its crew. With this in mind, Rue gathered the largest stones she could carry and began forging a distress signal along the clearing. While lifting a rock, barely set in the sand, a snake emerged from beneath it, and the wroth ophidian lashed out at her with its mouth agape and its fangs protruding from its jaws. Rue leaped backward to avoid the strike, and when it landed atop the sand, she drove the heel of her shoe down on its head. She did not lift her foot until the body stopped writhing. Rue draped the dead snake over her shoulder and finished forming the sign. When she was done, she returned to her camp to rest.

The next day was no less dull in appearance than the last, and Rue longed for even the slightest glimpse of sunlight. Once more, she bimbled throughout the graveyard of metal and wood until something she previously missed caught her eye. Beneath a pile of broken containers and dried weeds lay hidden a journal, unusual in appearance and composed of a sundry of papers. It had crinkled pages held together by small knots of fishing line which ran through crude holes punched along one side. A makeshift cover had been crafted from a cut piece of burlap, the same on which she had slept. The material was water-stained, and the faint smell of old tobacco clung to it. Of its many handmade pages, few contained any writing at all.

Rue found a small cache of other perishables tucked away with the journal. Some were of use, while others had succumbed to rot. She gathered the items and journal together in her arms and carried them and sat in the safety and quietude of her shrouded encampment. She read from the weather-worn pages of the improvised notebook.

Stranger's Journal

Entry 1.

This place is damned. I don't know how or why I'm here. I've been over it again and again in my mind, but I can't remember what happened. Only that I washed up after the ship sank. Things here make little sense. The sun never shines, and the days seem shorter than they should be. It looks as though this island is in a constant state of dusk, except at night when there's little light. Only, there's never a red dusk. Just a dark shade of gray. Gray and gray and depressing fucking gray. Am I dead? Is this what Hell is? Purgatory, perhaps? Nothing makes sense. Sometimes, I see things that look like ghosts, and I clutch the ring I wear around my neck. I don't know why. I think I was married once.

Entry 2.

I've been able to scavenge and make the most of what's on the beach. I think I can hold out here for a long while. I'm certainly not going into those woods. No way, no how. I swear it's cursed! I hear terrible things at night, and I have no weapons I can rely on. No, I'll wait here until a patrol finally comes along. Surely they'll come along, won't they?

Entry 3.

I should have known this place was evil. Those crows aren't just bad omens—they're the tools of devils! They're always watching. Always waiting. Always taunting me as they perch around my camp. They're sitting on top of this old lifeboat as I lay beneath it, writing these very words. They caw at me over and over and over again. But I won't listen to them. No sir.

Entry 4.

Those little beaked bastards! Stupid flying rats! The sand fleas had me itching this morning, so I bathed in the ocean. I folded my clothing, placed the pile on the beach, and set the wedding ring inside my shirt pocket. When I returned from the water, a crow landed on my things. It reached into my shirt pocket and pulled the ring up in its beak. Right in front of me! I ran as fast as I could, but it was too late—the little devil flew into the forest. I promise I'll get it back. I won't let this place keep the one connection I have to who I am.

After reading the journal, Rue packed it amongst the meager stock of provisions she had scavenged. She dozed as she rested by the fire. When she awoke, she saw through tired, blurry eyes that something was amiss. She blinked them clear again and looked around her campsite. Rue leaped to her feet in wild panic and stood trembling and aghast. The beach was devoid of its contents, and not even the fire was left to keep her warm; all that remained were the things in her jacket pockets.

Rue shambled along the shoreline in disbelief. She did not understand how a beach so cluttered with wreckage could suddenly become so void of it, but she knew that without fire or shelter or clean water, she would not last. The rain would only worsen, and whatever danger lurked in the forest was a risk she had no choice but to accept.

Angel

The verge of the wood line was staggered with exanimate trees that loomed throughout. Their twisted limbs were rangy and crooked, and they reached upwards into the somber sky above as though they were frightened children whose arms outstretched for a mother's embrace. Along the forest floor, a footpath had once been cut. In the absence of caretaking, the path had narrowed from foliage that crept over its peripheries, and the topsoil had transmuted to mire. Ravens flittered betwixt trees in cautious sweeps, like glances shared in the company of adroit hunters who stalk in guarded reticence.

Rue stood before the forest. She was pensive and uncertain, unable to see beyond the forest's forbidding tenebrosity. She pushed past her fear and strode along the path which ascended into the woods.

As she walked, the gaunt trees drew nearer together. The tighter they gathered, the less she could see of her surroundings. Even the whippoorwills had not the courage to call out to one another. Finding the silence strange, Rue looked up to where the tops of the trees formed in a circular pattern, and she thought it looked like an iris fixed around a soulless gray pupil. She wondered if the forest itself was watching her.

The woods grew darker with each step, and the air grew colder too. A clement fog rolled in, amassing until it enveloped the trees and everything between them. Rue could only see a short distance ahead of her. Regardless, she carried on, for there was nowhere else to go. She considered what she read in the journal. If she had washed up on an island, she hoped she might find help on the other side.

The narrow path widened, and Rue came upon a slight clearing within the woodlands. The ravens gathered in the surrounding trees like spectators in a coliseum, cheering or cawing; it was all the same. Rue looked to the right and saw a modest cabin, no bigger than a tool shed. It was built by hand from an assortment of cracked, moss-covered stones. Its door was made from pinewood and had since been marred by rot. Rue stepped forward, but another sight halted her in place.

Two creatures levitated a dozen feet above the forest floor. Their shapes seemed human, yet their rawboned bodies were unnatural and elongated and cloaked in robes, black and tattered. Upon their shoulders, where faces should have been, sat the peeled skulls of animals: a wolf and a ram. Between them, there sat a thorn-covered hill and staked into it like a flag raised to promulgate some secret and vile precept was a cross, inverted and minatory, for upon the cross, the disfigured corpse of a man hung upside down and his corvus-pecked entrails dangled from his eviscerated belly, and his heart had been wrenched from his chest and wedged sardonically into his mouth. Rue could not help but gasp. The phantoms let out a harrowing groan like that from another world, and Rue fled in terror into the stone cabin. When she slammed the wooden door behind her, she saw that a wrought iron latch was mounted to it. She slung the latch in place, locking it with trembling hands.

Rue crouched in the dark and covered her ears. She shut her eyes as the abominations rapped upon the door in a violent rage. When the knocking had stopped, she opened them again. She noticed the creased tips of well-worn boots peeking out from a shadowed corner of the room. Rue removed her hands from her ears, and the voice of a young woman spoke in a low whisper. "If you're not ready to die," she said, "don't let them see you, stupid."

"W-who's there?" Rue asked.

"Nobody."

"Who are you?"

"Does it really matter?"

"It matters."

The young woman paused and leaned out from the shadow. She had long black hair draped down over a single side of her wan face, and she glared at Rue with an inveterate perspicacity, not unlike a cat left forsaken who had long lived astray. From the corner of her mouth where her matte black lipstick had dried and cracked, she offered an elfin grin that masked her ruth. "Lyssa," she said skeptically, "And who the fuck are you?"

"Rue."

"Cute name."

"I guess."

"What brings you to hell, Rue?"

"I don't know."

"You don't know?"

"No, not really. I barely remember who I was, let alone how I got here. I woke up on a nearby beach, and strange things have happened to me ever since."

"That makes two of us."

"You don't know who you are?"

"No, and I don't know how I got here either."

Rue nodded. "Yesterday I found a journal," she said, "and whoever wrote it said this is an island. Is that true?"

"Yeah, I think so. That's why I came out here. I wanted to see what was in the direction you just came from."

"Nothing. More forest and shoreline after that."

"Oh."

"Sorry."

Lyssa shrugged. "Well, I guess that's that," she said.

"There's nothing where you came from?"

"There's a small town or a village—something like that. But it's abandoned."

"Abandoned?"

"Yeah."

"Is it safe?"

"No safer than this cabin."

"Are you going there next?"

"Might as well, since there's nowhere else to go."

"Then I'll go with you."

Lyssa studied Rue for a moment and nodded. "Okay," she said.

"Maybe we should wait until morning?"

"Yeah, we can leave in the morning."

Rue and Lyssa sat in the dark and rested until the faint light of the dreary morning outlined the rough edges of the cabin door. Lyssa dragged a tin bucket below an opening in the front wall. It was no larger than her hand might fit through. She stood atop the bucket, which wobbled beneath her feet as she extended her toes and peeked through the hole. "Are those things still out there?" Rue asked.

"I don't think so."

"I'm ready if you are."

"Yeah, me too."

"Okay."

Lyssa hopped down from the bucket and looked at Rue as though she might ask a question, but she hesitated. "What is it?" asked Rue.

"It's just—I don't suppose you've got any food?"

Rue reached into her jacket pocket and withdrew one of the granola bars. Lyssa's expression softened with genuine relief. When she took the bar, she tore away its foil and savored each bite like it was her last. Rue beheld the woman with solicitude. Lyssa ate, still surprised by Rue's kindness. She thanked her sheepishly. When she was finished, Rue unlatched the mechanism that held shut the door. They opened it together.

Though the creatures had gone, the crucified man remained there with them. Lyssa approached the corpse with an uncanny enchantment, gazing at the macabre spectacle before her. Rue felt apprehensive and stood back from it. When Lyssa saw this, she grabbed Rue's wrist and yanked her closer. "He's dead," Lyssa said. "There's nothing to be afraid of, so why are you acting like some scared little doe?"

"Because it's horrible," Rue replied. "How are you not bothered by this?"

Lyssa shrugged. "We all die someday, so why die a boring death?" she said, caressing the side of the man's mangled face in her palm. "His death wasn't boring. It was special."

"How can you say that about this poor man?"

"What makes you think he was innocent?" Lyssa lashed out. "What makes you think he wasn't a rapist or the kind of guy that fucked whimpering altar boys while their holier-than-thou parents sang hymns in the next room? Look around, Rue—there's something different about this place. Something supernatural. For all we know, this may be where we go to settle up on our sins. I can't remember mine, but I know they're there. I can feel them festering under the surface of my fucking skin. No one is so pure and faultless that they deserve a peaceful death, so we might as well embrace the violent ones when they find us."

Lyssa sighed. "So what about you?" she asked. "Are you really so innocent?"

"I don't know what I am."

"But you feel it too, don't you?"

"Yes."

"I thought so."

Rue paused for a moment, trading embittered glares with Lyssa. Yet the desire for peace made her shift the conversation in another direction. "Did you see it happen?"

Lyssa shook her head. "No," she said, "he was like this when I got here. That was around ten minutes or so before we met in the cabin."

"Do you think they were waiting?"

"It's possible. Could have followed one of us too."

Rue's gaze became fixated on an item hanging from the neck of the dead man: a wedding ring attached to a single string. She thought of the journal she found and recalled that the man who wrote it spoke of losing such a thing.

"We should get going," Lyssa said.

"Yeah, okay."

Rue and Lyssa continued along the forest path. Lyssa led, for she already knew the way. The cool brume suffused the ground and the trees, and it left nothing untouched. Damp leaves lay blanketing the soft soil beneath their feet, quieting their steps as they walked. Rue thought it might lessen their chances of being heard. Here and there, she noticed the outlying vestiges of ancient structures looming above twisted patches of thickets and brush, and it seemed as if they had been cast aside by time itself. Though she pondered the dark histories that may lie hidden beneath the foundations of the old frameworks, she also feared them.

The trees began to grow apart. Rue became hopeful that she and Lyssa had reached the end of the forest. In a brief moment of reverie, she breathed a sigh of relief. Lyssa paused at the edge of the wood line. The moment was gone. Rue felt anything but ease.

Beyond the woods stood a pair of incomplete transmission towers, rusted and powerless. Sagging steel cables ran between them. Dangling from the arms of the towers, there hung a medley of withered corpses, some big and some small, and while many were clothed in threadbare coverings, others swayed in their naked form. All had been long forgotten and left to stagnate. In the zephyr of the island air, the twisting of the ropes that held the bodies made an off-rhythm cacophony of creaks and moans like the tenuous shifting of the limbs of the forest trees. "Did all these people kill themselves?" Rue wondered aloud.

"Maybe," said Lyssa, "but that's not an easy climb."

"You think those things in the woods put them there?"

"Probably, yeah."

"Maybe it's some kind of warning."

"I don't think so, little doe."

"Then what are they there for?"

"Decoration."

Rue looked at Lyssa, expecting to see a mischievous grin across her pale face, but in her expression, there was no humor at all, and Rue knew she was giving a wholehearted opinion on the matter. "There's an old church ahead," Lyssa pointed out. "We should probably think about hunkering down before it gets dark again."

"Good idea," Rue agreed.

"The town or village or whatever you want to call it is just past it. We can check it out tomorrow morning."

"Is there anything to eat or drink in the church?"

"I don't know. I've only passed it once and didn't go inside."

"Did it not look worth searching?"

Lyssa shook her head. "It wasn't that," she said.

"What was it?"

"I just don't like them."

"You don't like churches?"

"No."

"Okay."

Lyssa thought for a moment and then continued. "Why? Do you like churches?" she asked.

"I don't think I feel any way about them, but I guess I'm a little wary of any religious place abandoned on a haunted island."

"Haunted but empty might not be so bad."

"You don't think abandoned churches are creepy enough as it is?"

"That's the thing—it's not churches that scare me."

"So, what is it then?"

"It's the people inside them."

Rue looked at Lyssa and nodded. She thought that something in Lyssa's past had wounded her in the deepest of ways, and whatever it was was the kind of hurt that made her admire the dead yet fear the place where souls are said to be saved.

The women came upon the old church as evening crept over the isle. Beside it was a little cemetery where stone graves stood, cracked and crumbling, and their elegant engravings had evanesced like the bygone occupants beneath them. Interspersed between the headstones lay new plots. They had crosses made of sticks to mark them. Some of the fresh plots were filled with loose dirt, while others were empty and uncovered. Lyssa peaked over the edge of the nearest of the open graves and motioned for Rue to come to see it. Rue shook her head. Lyssa waved her hand dismissively as she continued to study what lay inside.

Rue approached the church. It was modest and unadorned aside from the remnants of stained glass windows. The white outer walls were blackened and singed as if set aflame yet extinguished before the fire could damage their integrity. A short set of stairs went up to the church's double doors, which were tall and still intact. There were gashes and scrapes along them, and Rue wondered what might have caused such marks.

When Rue pushed on the left door, it did not budge, so she leaned her shoulder into the right. It creaked open, not more than a few inches. Lyssa stood at the bottom of the stairs and waited. Rue cautiously peeked inside, but it was too dark to see. She pushed open the door the rest of the way and stepped forward, and using the glow of the flame from her lighter, she walked into the sanctuary. The pews had been moved around, and some were turned over on their sides. The floor beneath her feet was coated in thick dust. Illuminated there in the flickering of the flame, there lay the fragments of stained glass strewn about, glimmering like stars upon the sea.

Rue continued to explore the room as Lyssa stayed close to her. "Ouch!" Rue exclaimed, dropping the lighter on the floor.

"What happened?"

"The metal thumb wheel got too hot, and I touched it by accident."

"You're a fuckin clutz," Lyssa teased. "You know that?"

"Sorry, can you help me find it?"

"I think it's over here somewhere. I felt it bounce off of my boot."

"Careful when you find it. It's probably still hot."

Lyssa crawled in the dark on hands and knees and stretched out her fingers and slid them along the gritty floor. When she felt the plastic casing brush against her fingertips, she snatched it up. "Found it!" she proclaimed. She ran her thumb down over the metal striker wheel. When the flame lashed out from the hood of the lighter, it cast wild shadows against the sanctuary's walls. The women crouched in the dark, and a face lurked between them. Its features twisting and contorting in the dance of the flame. The women screamed. Rue leaped to her feet, and Lyssa fell backward onto her rear. Mustering what courage she could, Lyssa brought the lighter closer to where the face had been. She laughed, and Rue laughed too. The terrible thing that scared them was not terrible at all; a statue of an angel had been set there long before their arrival. "I think my soul just packed up and left this universe," Rue said.

"If ever there's a good time to see an angel, I guess this is it."

"I'm starting to think there aren't enough underpants in the world to get us through this experience."

"Our final words will be, 'We literally can't take this shit anymore.'"

Rue grinned, but the bitterness of reality seeped back into her mind. "We should search the rest of the church while there's still fluid left in the lighter," she said.

Lyssa nodded, and they continued to explore the building. The church only consisted of four rooms. The door to the first room was locked and would not budge. Next to it was a study with only enough space for a desk and a bookshelf. A walk-in storage closet stood across from the study, and it had been converted into a pantry. At the end of the hall, there was a bathroom. Lyssa opened the bathroom door. A nun was sitting, slouched against the wall. Her body was long rotted and decayed. Wrists face up and covered with dried blood. It had flowed from her wounds and pooled beneath her in the final moments of her life. Rue shivered and looked away. "Did she—"

"Yeah," Lyssa answered.

"I thought they didn't believe in that."

"They don't."

Rue tried again to look upon the horrible sight but could not. She wondered what terrors might make a person risk sacred eternity to avoid a moment of suffering and found the absence of a reason unnerving.

The women moved to the pantry, where there were racks along each wall. On the shelves, they found several cans of fruit and vegetables. A tinplate container held a dozen ounces of corned beef. There were dried noodles and bottles of juice and water. Many of the items were packaged with labels printed in different languages. Rue pointed to a top shelf. "I think I see some blankets and towels up there," she said. "We can use them to keep warm tonight."

Lyssa nodded and noticed something next to her. "Is this really what I think it is?" she asked. She picked up a flashlight. It was hung by a lanyard from a bent nail in the wall.

"Does it work?"

"Doesn't look like it. Maybe the batteries are dead."

A look of realization came over Rue. "Wait, try these," she said.

Rue reached into her jacket pocket and removed the batteries she had found on the beach. She gave them to Lyssa and took back the lighter. Lyssa unscrewed the bottom of the flashlight's handle, and three batteries, all drained of their energy, slid out from the interior compartment. She replaced each one and turned it on. Its beam, dull and colorless, shot down at the floor and flooded the bottom of the pantry with light. "Holy shit, it works," Lyssa said.

"I've been carrying those batteries around for a while," Rue replied. "I thought they might come in handy."

"That was smart."

"Thanks."

"Let's take a few things and settle in for the night."

"Sounds good to me. Where do you want to sleep?"

"I guess we can camp out in the other room."

"Okay."

Rue and Lyssa gathered what provisions they could carry in their thin arms and lugged them into the sanctuary and piled them in the corner of the room. Lyssa checked the doors to ensure they were locked while Rue collected flat cushions from broken pews. She thought the cushions might help them sleep through the night on the hardwood floor. When Lyssa returned, the women laid down together. They huddled like animals, denning in the dark as soft moonlight broke through the clouds. It glistened along the edges of the shattered windows. The women satiated their hunger and their thirst in the dim, wobbling glow of a single candle they borrowed from an altar. Vague memories trickled into their weary minds, but still, they struggled to remember their pasts. Rue and Lyssa stayed beneath the blankets. They talked. They compared their experiences on the island. They speculated on what they might find down in the village. Then, they went to sleep.

In the quiet of the night, a man's voice whispered in Rue's ear. She jolted awake. Her eyes scanned the room, and she was afraid that someone had come to harm them while they slept. She shook Lyssa and tried to rouse her, but Lyssa did not wake. "Who's there?" Rue called out. A tall man, striking in appearance, stepped forward into the timid moonlight. Rue pleaded, "Leave us alone!"

"Rue, don't be afraid," he said soothingly.

"How do you know my name?"

"I've always known you."

Rue shook Lyssa again without taking her eyes off the stranger. "She can't feel or hear you right now," the man said.

"What do you mean?"

"She and I are speaking at this very moment, but to her, you are the one who's asleep."

"That's not possible."

"Not all are bound by the rules you perceive of time and space, Rue."

"I don't understand."

"You will, someday."

"You said that you've always known me. Can you tell me who I am or how I got here?"

"I can't tell you everything you want to know, but I assure you that your memories will be restored. For now, I can only point you in the right direction."

"What do you mean?"

"There's an asylum not far beyond the village. Keep going past it until you reach a house that stands alone in a meadow."

"What will I find there?"

"Your truth."

"What about Lyssa?"

"She'll find hers too—but in a different place, in a different way."

"Will you come with us?"

The man shook his head.

"Oh," Rue said. "Will we meet again?"

"We will meet again."

"What's your nam—"

In a blink of Rue's tired eyes, the man was gone. She sat in the cold dark of night with a single word on her lips, a name she never knew until now. "Riel," she whispered.

In the morning, the smell of stale tobacco and cheap booze entered Rue's nostrils, and she saw that Lyssa was awake. She had found a stash of whiskey and cigarettes inside a desk drawer in the priest's study. "A blessing, isn't it?" Lyssa said, gesturing with a lit cigarette. She scrutinized Rue from the corner of her eye and examined the label of the whiskey bottle. "Maybe this shit's made with real 100-proof holy water."

"Maybe you're right," Rue replied. "Maybe it is a blessing."

Lyssa rolled her eyes. "I'm just saying," continued Rue, "sometimes the smallest miracles get us through the worst times, and the worst times make those small miracles feel bigger than any other."

"I thought you were innocent, little doe, but not that innocent. Maybe you haven't noticed that this isn't the kind of place where faith and optimism have done anyone any good, or else they'd still be here. Smiling and alive. Not dead on some bathroom floor."

"Yeah, maybe."

Lyssa took an indulgent drag from the cigarette and exhaled a thin white cloud into the air. "You saw him last night, too?" she asked.

"Yeah."

"At least I'm not completely crazy then."

Rue shook her head. "What did he tell you?" she asked.

"Some bullshit about 'finding my truth.'"

Lyssa threw the cigarette down on the ground and snuffed it out with a twist of her boot. She smeared the ash across the floor as if in spite.

"You don't think it's worth trying?" asked Rue.

"I don't think it matters."

"Why wouldn't it?"

"Because I don't need to remember who I am to know my life wasn't worth an ounce of dogshit to begin with."

"Don't say that."

"Tell me, where does he want you to go?"

"A house in a meadow."

"A house?"

Rue nodded. "What about you?" she asked.

"An asylum, Rue. My truth is in a fucking asylum."

Rue and Lyssa sat in uncomfortable silence. They made a meager breakfast from the supplies they had scavenged. Afterward, they lined their pockets with as much as they could take with them. Rue pushed open the sanctuary doors and heard a dog bark somewhere in the distance but thought perhaps her mind was playing tricks on her. Lyssa took the lead once more.

When the women came upon a valley, they stood there overlooking it. They saw sundry decrepit buildings and ramshackle houses from a part of history they never knew. They looked at each other and nodded and climbed down from the ridge on which they stood, descending into the village below.

Survivors

The path to the village snaked beneath the ridge. It sloped to one side due to the shifting of soil after countless years of rain and neglect. Rue and Lyssa made their way down with careful attention to each step, and it was not long before they came to a road. Upon the road, no vehicle could be seen, save for the skeletal frame of a single antiquated truck, thick with crimson rust.

Where the path and the road met were two wooden posts. Between them hung a mutilated cadaver. It was strung up with its left wrist bound to one post and its right wrist attached to the other. Hundreds of cuts were made to the arms and torso. From the feet to the waist, it appeared that animals had devoured what once had been a living person. Atop the corpse's drooping head, a raven sat pecking flies from the scalp, and when the women approached, it spread its wings and flew away. "Ugh, I hate those things," Rue said. She covered her face with her palm, attempting to reduce the effect of the putrid odor. "They freak me out."

"I think they're beautiful," Lyssa replied.

"I think they're weird."

"Maybe you think that because people only choose to see them as bad omens. You might seem weird too if you were constantly judged for what people wanted to believe about you and not for who you are."

"Sure, that's fair. I guess I never thought of it like that."

Lyssa paused and stared into the distance as if lost in thought. "Never underestimate the audacity of judgmental people," she continued. "They're like vampires who feed on everyone around them, and when it's time to account for their own flaws, they can stare at a mirror for hours and still never see their reflection."

Rue nodded. "Speaking of spooky creatures of the night, what do you think tore into this person?" she asked as she inspected the carcass.

"Definitely something larger than ravens."

"Or maybe one giant raven."

"You're getting my hopes up."

Rue opened her mouth to reply but stopped when she noticed that the head of the cadaver moved in an unnatural way. "What the hell?" she asked. "Tell me you saw that."

"The head moved by itself."

"Why did it move?"

"You're asking me?"

"What if they're still alive?"

"I doubt that."

"What do we do?"

"Lift the head and check the face—if there's even a face to check."

"You're making me do it?"

"Yeah."

"You can fuck off. You know that?"

"Hey, don't threaten me with a good time."

"Ugh, shut up and let's get this over with."

Rue pulled her hand up into her sleeve and used the loose end to grab hold of the corpse's grotty hair. Despite her revulsion, she lifted its head. As its face rose, a throng of writhing maggots poured from the mouth and cavum and sockets in spasmodic bursts. A swarm of scarlet flies fulminated from the orifices, plunging through the air like wasps. The insects bit ferociously anywhere skin was exposed. The women screamed and fled from the cadaver. They ran until the swarm ceased its attack. Rue and Lyssa stopped to catch their breaths in front of a cluster of storefronts, immemorial in design. Echoing nearby from within the village were the yips and barks and howling of dogs.

Before the women could think of their next move, a man dashed out from a deserted leather shop across from where they stood. He pushed one finger against his lips to hush them, and Rue froze, uncertain of what she should do. The man grabbed her wrist and said something in Japanese, but she did not understand him. "Hey!" Lyssa shouted. "Get your fuckin hands off her!" She lunged forward and swung a tight fist. It struck him at the corner of his left eye. Surprised by the sudden impact, he staggered backward and let go of Rue's wrist. Lyssa positioned herself between them and drew something from inside her jacket. She had crafted a knife in secret from a broken shard of stained glass, the lower portion wrapped with strips of fabric to fashion a handle. She gripped the weapon and pointed the blade toward the stranger. "Try that shit again," she warned, "and I'll go for your neck or your nuts. You pick."

"Calm down!" the man hissed. "You've got the wrong idea. I'll explain in a minute, but first, we need to get inside. They're coming!"

"It's okay," Rue said to Lyssa, "let's just go with him."

"Please, we can't stay here!" the man urged.

Lyssa shot a rankled glare at Rue. "Fine," she replied through gritted teeth.

The man gestured toward the leather shop from which he had emerged. He followed the women as they rushed inside. They leaped over the jagged panes of the shop's shattered windows, and the howling and yipping grew louder behind them. Rue could hear the dense thuds of massive paws stampeding upon the road, scratching through moist dirt and against broken cobblestone. Rue ran through a door at the back of the main room and spun around on her heels. She saw a hellish pack of feral dogs skidding to the front of the store. Possessed by some wickedness, not of this world, for their eyes were soulless and dull like sea glass. Their fur was matted with blood. Patches of skin were exposed from legions and mange. The man slipped through the door, and the hounds charged at him in a blind rage. They howled and snarled, and viscid drool and foam flung from their gnashing teeth.

As they lunged toward the man, he slammed shut the door and bolted its lock. "What the hell?" asked Rue. "Were those dogs?"

"You're asking the wrong guy," the man answered.

"Yeah, about that," said Lyssa. "Who the hell are you, anyway?"

The man chuckled under his breath and put his back to the door, sliding down into a squat. "Is that funny?" Lyssa asked.

"No, it's just..." He paused and stared at the floor, searching for the right word. "Ironic," he said.

"How is that ironic?" Rue replied.

"Because even though I'm 'the guy,' you're still asking the wrong guy."

"You've got to be shitting me," said Lyssa. "Another amnesia case."

"I guess that makes three of us."

"Six, actually," the man added. "I met a few others. We've been hiding out in the building behind this one."

"They don't remember who they are either?" asked Rue

"No, none of us do. We remember our names. Maybe some random things that probably don't matter, but not much more than that."

"So what's your name then?" Lyssa replied.

"Makoto, or Koto if you prefer."

"It's nice to meet you, Koto," Rue answered. Lyssa nodded reluctantly but said nothing.

"If you want to join me and the others, you're more than welcome to. The odds are better if we all stick together."

"Until you start eating each other," Lyssa said sarcastically.

"We scavenged a fair amount of supplies, so I think we're off each others' menus for a while."

"There you go, Rue—delayed cannibalism. Must be one of those small miracles of yours." Rue ignored the jab.

"If you don't mind me asking, how long have you two been on the island?"

"Four—maybe five days?" Rue answered. "You?"

"Three days."

"Have any of you been outside the village?"

"Each of us woke up on our own, but we all started near or along the shoreline. One by one, we wandered into the village from different directions. On our first night together, we found a safe place to hide. Barely left it since. Not with those things roaming out there."

"You said you each woke up on different shorelines. This must really be an island, after all."

"Far as we can tell."

"Have you seen anything else?"

"Like what?"

"Like—"

"Ghosts," Lyssa said.

Makoto nodded. He, too, had seen apparitions and agreed that their intentions were malignant and vile. "We steer clear of them," he said. "In Japan, where I came from, I grew up hearing stories about kami, or spirits as you call them. But I never thought they were real. I guess I was wrong." A moment of mutual sentiment was shared between the three survivors, but the instinct to press on swelled inside their minds. "When the dogs are gone, I'll go back to the others," Makoto said. "You should come too."

Rue looked at Lyssa, who shook her head. She shrugged disapprovingly, but Rue turned back to Makoto and nodded. "We'll go with you," she said. Lyssa bit her lip in frustration.

Makoto watched through a window in the rear door of the leather shop. He waited for the dogs to lose interest in their hunt. Rue and Lyssa maundered about the room, intrigued by items that were foreign to them. There were scraps of leather for crafting, much of which had dried out. Set against a wall, there leaned tanning racks on which hides were stretched from end to end. Upon a workbench, spread across like some exquisite banquet set atop a dining table, there lay materials and needles and thread and tools and glue; projects started once upon a time but never finished.

An hour passed before Makoto gestured that it was safe to leave. He unlatched the lock on the door and opened it in slow, careful movements. In a quiet maneuver, he crossed the alley. The women followed behind him, watching in every direction. When they reached the rear of the neighboring building, Makoto pulled open a metal door. One after the other, they went inside. The door shut with a dull, reverberant clank. A thick layer of soft white powder coated the floor and muted each step they took. At the edge of a countertop, Rue noticed a large sack of flour had been tipped over. They were standing in a bakery. It was cold and dark and void of cakes or desserts or confectionary delights, aside from some dried crumbs that even the insects had rejected. To Rue's disappointment, the place smelled anything but delightful.

A hefty baker's rack was set against a wall. Makoto slid it a few feet to one side, revealing another door. He opened it and ushered Rue and Lyssa through and then followed. Makoto closed the door, leaving only a few inches of space between its edge and frame. A rope, assembled from frayed, oily rags, had been tied between the inner handle and the baker's rack, and he used it to return the rack to the front of the door from the inside. He clicked the door into place and locked it.

There was nowhere to go but up a single flight of stairs. When they reached the top, they entered a living space. It was long unused yet warmer than anywhere they had been so far. At a table, there sat a man and a woman. The woman smiled; there was kindness in her eyes. The man at the table said nothing at all. Another man stood leaning against a tall armoire. He was older than the rest and was reading a book that he shut and placed back on a shelf. Stacked along a wall were scavenged provisions, including food and clean water and candles. There were loose papers meant for toiletry. The windows were covered with articles of clothing that had been torn and stretched across to keep candlelight from being seen from outside. "Hey, what do we got here?" the old man asked with a southern drawl.

"Two more like us," Makoto replied.

The woman at the table rose from her seat and spoke another language as she greeted them. Rue shook her head. "I'm so sorry—I don't understand," she said.

"Sadly, we don't neither." the old man replied. "Faina here is Russian, and she don't speak any English. She does sign, though, if any of y'all know how to sign. Rest of us can't."

"Oddly enough, now that we're talking about it, I think I recall knowing some sign language. ASL, I think. But that's not the same as Russian Sign Language, so I don't know if it will work."

"Can't hurt to try."

The old man looked at Faina and gestured at Rue. "Do you want to try signin?" he asked out loud, so the others would understand. Faina thought for a moment and then raised her hands and signed something to Rue.

"It's ASL," Rue said, relieved. "I'm not sure why she knows it over her native version, but she does."

"Well, I reckon now you can ask her."

Rue moved her fingers and hands in fluid motions and found that signing was natural to her. She asked Faina how she came to learn a language of signing different from that of her home country. Faina thought that perhaps a loved one from America had taught it to her. It was only a guess, but it was her best guess. It was good enough for Rue.

"What about y'all?" the man asked. "What do we call y'all?"

"This is Rue and this is Lyssa," Makoto said as he gestured to one and then the other. He turned toward the older man. "This is Cody. You already met Faina. And that's Dolion there at the table." Dolion nodded.

Lyssa slinked to the corner of the room. She stayed silent as the group made small talk, and Rue could sense her discomfort. She knew that Lyssa was wary and cynical. She was at ease in solitude, but now she was surrounded by others. Rue asked Makoto if there was a place where they could rest in private. He showed them to a spare bedroom, and Faina took from the group's supplies two blankets and a candle and placed them inside. Rue thanked her. When they entered the room, Lyssa shut the door and locked it behind them. "I'm not okay with this," she said angrily in a low whisper.

"Okay with what?"

"Staying here with these strangers."

"Why not? They seem like good people."

Lyssa glared at Rue, a stinging disappointment in her eyes. "You're telling yourself that because it's what you want to believe. You're too afraid to consider the possibility that these aren't good people because, deep down, you don't want to be alone."

"That's not true."

"Really? Because you're clearly tough on your own, or else you wouldn't have survived for all those days before we met. But when someone else is around, you just fall in line, right? No backbone, just a human doormat."

"What? No, I don't know what you're—"

"You know exactly what I'm talking about, Rue. When I showed up, you followed me without question. You never challenged me on anything I said. Then, some strange man comes out of nowhere and grabs you, and four seconds later, there you are, on your way to meet his family. You didn't even stop to consider that your passiveness—your naivety—might put me at risk right along with you."

Rue stood there, hurt and silent. She took in the accusation, and though she could not say why, she knew Lyssa was right. She could feel it deep inside of her. "I'm sorry, Lys," she said. "I didn't mean to make you feel that way. You're not wrong. That's something I need to work on."

"It's okay," Lyssa replied. She let out a sigh. "I'm just trying to keep us safe."

"I know. And even though we only just met, I'm glad you're my friend. I hope you know that."

Lyssa paused and looked awkwardly at the floor. "Thanks. It's been a long time since I had one of those."

Rue stepped in toward Lyssa, and Lyssa's body tensed. She hugged her anyway. When Lyssa felt the embrace, she relaxed. She wrapped her arms around Rue's back, bringing them up from beneath the underside of her arms and over the back of her shoulders. She nestled her face into Rue's neck. She inhaled in a slow and tranquil way. She did this because, despite the absence of her memories, she knew she had not felt a human connection for a time beyond what she could measure. Her eyes welled, and a tear ran down her cheek. She wiped it away with her sleeve but did not let Rue see.

The women left the spare room and stepped back into the central area of the living space. They joined the others who were dividing their evening meal amongst themselves. Cody and Faina handed generous portions to Rue and Lyssa, and the group huddled together as unkempt vagabonds, clinging to the tiniest pleasures they had left. They discussed everything, from their experiences on the island to their theories about it. More importantly, how they might escape. "Has anyone met a guy named Riel?" Rue asked.

"We've all seen him, but never at the same time," answered Cody. "Come while we was asleep and scared the ever-lovin shit out of us."

"He came to us too," Lyssa replied. "Told us to go to different places where we could each find answers."

"He told us this as well," Makoto said.

"Where did he send the rest of you?" asked Rue.

"Well, we ain't gone nowhere just yet," Cody replied, "but we mean to. I'm supposed to go to a tavern round the corner from here, but Koto's meant to go to some house with a black door and Faina a clinic. Sounds kinda crazy though, don't it?"

"No crazier than anything else we've seen so far," Rue said.

"What about you?" Lyssa asked, looking at Dolion. There was an awkward pause.

"He ain't never seen Riel," Cody answered, "at least not yet, anyway."

Dolion shook his head. "He's not gonna bother with me," he said.

"Why's that?" Lyssa asked skeptically. "Why speak with everyone here but you?"

"Because this is a place of devilry. Isn't it obvious? Only those who serve the Lord can be saved from it. I'm a man of God, and if Riel is a man of God, he won't bother to offer me guidance I don't need. If he's not a man of God, he's in alignment with the enemy, so there'd be no point in me listening to him."

"I'm sorry, but how would either of you know what the other believes if you've never spoken before?"

"Excuse me?"

"You're assuming an awful lot about a guy you've never met."

"Are you calling me a liar?"

"Your word choice, but hey, let's go with it."

"Do you even know who you're talking to? Waltzing in here with your rebellious clothing and your piercings and your bad attitude, and you have the gall to question me?" Dolion scoffed. "This whole act," he continued, "let me just say it isn't becoming of a woman. In fact, looking at you, I'd say your chances of getting out of this place are awfully slim."

"Yeah, cool, but instead of deflecting, how about you answer my question, you self-righteous fucktwat—or did God not give you the guts to be honest?"

"I'm not a liar, and frankly, your question no longer warrants a response." Dolion stood up and stormed into another room, slamming the door behind him. Lyssa furrowed her brow.

"You're not wrong to ask," Makoto whispered. "We were wondering the same thing."

"It's fine," Lyssa replied. "I know I can be a bit—"

"Prickly?" Cody asked with a slight chuckle behind the word.

"Yeah."

"It ain't nothin to us, darlin. We get it. This whole damn situation's got us all on edge."

"It's just that I'm always angry and don't know why. I don't mean to take it out on anyone—I just snap sometimes."

"I reckon there's a lot about us we won't understand until we get our memories back."

"So let's talk about getting them back," Makoto said.

Everyone nodded in agreement except for Faina, who did not understand. *What did he say?* she signed.

He said let's talk about getting our memories back, Rue replied. She continued to sign throughout the conversation so Faina could follow.

"I don't think rescue is coming," Makoto said.

"Why not?" Rue asked.

"Because if anyone knew about this place, it would be crawling with scientists and experts, not isolated and littered with corpses."

"Plus, there ain't no fast food," Cody joked. "Ain't no lived-in place on earth where there ain't fast food close by."

"I hate how much sense that made," Lyssa replied, failing to hold back a smirk.

Faina signed again, to which Rue translated, "She wants to know how we feel about following Riel's instructions?"

"If rescue isn't coming, there's no point in trying to wait this out," Makoto answered. "All we can do is try to find a way to escape. Under normal circumstances, it would make sense to reject what Riel is saying, but these aren't normal circumstances. We might have to take our chances and listen to what he's telling us."

"We each were told to go somewhere different, and I think we should do exactly that," replied Rue, "but together, as one group. What else can we do besides wait until we starve to death or get killed by those monsters?"

"I agree with both of y'all," Cody said. Lyssa and Faina each nodded.

"Then it's settled," Makoto replied. "We'll leave at dawn and cover as much ground as possible. Maybe we'll find our way home after all—wherever that is."

The others slept in the master bedroom while Rue and Lyssa stayed in the spare room. In the corner of the room was an old wood bed frame. There was a stain shaped like a rood on the wall above it, and Rue wondered where the crucifix had gone. As candlelight flickered in the dark, the women drew close to one another. They were eager to soak up each other's warmth beneath the blankets.

In the night, Rue dreamed the first good dream since her stranding. She stood in the middle of a great city of light. There was a vague feeling, and that feeling was hope. When she woke from the dream, it was still dark. Still cold. She thought she heard some terrible cry outside the window. The uncertainty of it nagged at her, and she struggled to fall back asleep. She rolled out from under Lyssa's arm, attempting not to wake her. Rue noticed the stained-glass dagger in Lyssa's clenched hand. *Protective even in her sleep*, she thought. *I wish I could be like that.*

Rue saw a faint glow beneath the spare room door. She crept into the central area to see who was awake. There at the table, Faina sat sipping tea she had warmed over a flame. *Would you like some?* Faina signed. *I think it's decaf.*

I'd love some, Rue replied.

Faina poured the tea into a faded porcelain cup and handed it to Rue. *Thank you*, she said.

Faina smiled. *Sorry I don't talk much. It's hard to do when no one understands you.*

Sometimes I feel like—even when people understand me—they don't understand me.

Faina giggled, covering her mouth to keep from waking the others. *Yes, I know exactly what you mean,* she said.

Are you sure you're okay with the plan for tomorrow?

I think it's the only way we can move forward, and, like all of us, I need to get back to wherever home is. Not just for me, but because... Faina hesitated as she fought back tears. *I think I might be a mother.*

What makes you say that? Do you remember something from your past?

Not exactly.

Faina lifted her shirt with one hand and lowered the waistband of her pants with the other. Rue saw what looked to be a scar from where an infant had been delivered through the abdomen. "Faina!" she said, struggling to contain her surprise.

When I first noticed, I was shocked and confused and scared. Then, I felt guilty for not remembering the birth of my own child. Now, all I want is to find them.

You'll get out of here, Faina—we all will.

Faina stood up and hugged Rue. *Thank you,* she said. *I can't tell you how happy I am that we can speak like this.*

Me too. I just wish I could remember how I learned it in the first place.

I guess we should get what rest we can before morning. With any luck, we'll finally get some answers. Rue nodded and helped Faina tidy up the table. A shriek echoed again somewhere in the village.

Did you hear that? Rue asked.

Yes.

What was that?

The ghouls that roam the island torture the dogs at night. We aren't sure if it's meant to get in our heads or simply for their sick enjoyment. On our first night here, they did it so close to the bakery that we had to cover our ears for hours.

That's awful.

Faina shook her head. *Try not to let it get to you, okay?*

Okay.

Goodnight, Rue.

Goodnight.

Rue snuck back into the spare room. She tried her best to avoid creaky floorboards. Lyssa was still asleep, and Rue thought that she looked at peace. She sat on the edge of the bed, and in slow, careful movements, she laid down and slid back into her friend's embrace.

"Where'd you go?" Lyssa asked, her eyes still shut.

"I couldn't sleep. I think I just needed to clear my head for a minute."

"Please don't leave me, little doe."

"I won't."

"Promise?"

"I promise."

"Okay."

Hope

W hen the next gray dawn approached, there was a knock on the bedroom door. Makoto asked Rue and Lyssa to prepare for the trek through the village. They got ready, and when they finished, they gathered with the rest of the group. The survivors ate oatmeal and dry cereal and filled their pockets with food to take with them as they explored the isle. They decided their first destination would be the old tavern, where Riel had instructed Cody to seek his truth. It was closest to the bakery, and from there, they would search the village for the next of their assigned locations.

On the lower floor, Makoto studied the road in front of the bakery. He watched for signs of dogs or other creatures lurking out in the mist. Behind him, the survivors waited. Dolion glared at Lyssa. She crossed her arms and looked away. "I'm sorry if I offended you," he said. "I think we got off on the wrong foot last night."

"Sure, don't worry about it," replied Lyssa.

"I do worry."

"Worry about what?"

"About your soul, and your friend Rue's soul and Makoto's and everyone else's."

"Did it ever occur to you that maybe our souls ain't yours to save?" Cody asked.

"I'm a Christian, Cody. I know that our purpose in this life is to save as many souls as we can before it's too late."

"That ain't true, and you damn well know it. I was raised in the church too, and was taught from the same Bible you were. If we're called to do anything, it's to share God's love with folks and that Jesus died for em, and that's it. The rest is up to Him and them. We ain't God's enforcers, and we ain't His soul collectors, neither. So do us all a favor and don't pretend to be our friend just so you can try to boost your spiritual ego, alright? I don't take kindly to it. None of us do."

Dolion's face flooded with red. He huffed and walked to the other side of the room. As he did, Cody saw that Rue had been standing behind Dolion the whole time. She was signing the conversation to Faina, who tried her hardest not to laugh. "Keepin Faina up on the drama, I see," he said. Rue shrugged and grinned mischievously.

"Thanks," Lyssa said. "You didn't have to stick up for me."

"Nah, don't mention it," Cody replied. "Shit like that just rubs me the wrong way, is all."

Lyssa gave a slight smile.

Makoto continued watching the road. Time passed, and he thought that perhaps the island's ghostly inhabitants were distracted elsewhere. He motioned for everyone to follow him toward the tavern. As they crept along the road, they heard an unfamiliar voice call out ahead. A language none spoke. Without a word, they concluded with unanimity that this person was yet another strandee like them, perhaps unknowing of the isle's malicious nature. Hiding behind broken carts and wooden crates and alongside shopfronts, they observed. A man came forth from the fog. Just as quickly as he came, he was gone. Snatched back into the fog by some creature that reached out without a sound, like an arachnid catching prey. It was the last of him they had ever heard or seen.

The group continued, maneuvering around and behind buildings to avoid spending too much time on the road. Soon, they approached the rear of the tavern. The door was locked. A narrow opening above the door was large enough that a person small in frame might fit through it. Makoto leaned against the door and laced together his fingers. "You're the smallest," he said, looking at Rue.

"It's moments like these when being the short one stops being cute," she replied.

Makoto raised her to where she could grab hold of the ledge, and she pulled herself inside. She landed on the other side of the door and dusted off her pants and shoulders and unlocked the metal bolt. It rolled to the right, grinding dirt and rust along the interior cylinder as it clicked into place. Makoto opened the door and stepped through. The others followed single file.

Cody became uneasy when they entered the barroom. Lyssa was elated. She scampered behind the bar like a child approaching gifts on Christmas morning, wide-eyed and gleeful. She found that a tall bottle of whiskey and a single glass tumbler had been set atop a short stack of letters. Lifting the bottle, she saw that the pages were composed of feminine handwriting addressed to women she did not know.

"These might have something to do with why we're here," said Lyssa to Cody as she gestured at the letters with the bottle in her hand. She poured the whiskey into the lowball glass and slid it toward him, the brown liquid sloshing from side to side. "Do those letters look like anything to you?"

Cody took a deep breath and sat at the bar, holding the letters in his trembling hands. Faina noticed his distress and sat next to him. She put her hand on his shoulder, and Lyssa admired her empathy. "What's wrong?" Rue asked.

"I got a feelin pickin em up," Cody answered. "There's just a heaviness about em, deep down inside me. I ain't sure how to explain it."

While Cody mustered the courage to read the letters, Dolion and Makoto sat at a dirty card table. Rue sat at the other end of the bar. Lyssa pulled five more glasses from beneath the counter and poured whiskey into each one. She handed the first two to Rue and Faina. The third to Makoto. When she offered the fourth glass to Dolion, he declined.

"I don't drink," he said, waving his hand dismissively.

"Of course you don't," Lyssa replied. She sucked down the extra drink in one gulp and slammed the empty glass face-down on the table. Dolion rolled his eyes.

A scrawny black cat brushed against Lyssa's leg and let out an affectionate meow. Bewildered at its sudden appearance, each survivor glanced about the room to see where it might have come from. Lyssa petted its head in short, soft strokes. It looked up at her with its viridescent eyes and purred.

Cody began to read from the letters. When he saw the first few words, he reached out to Faina, who held his hand. Tears welled in his eyes. His throat tightened. It came in stages: familiarity, memories, and truth.

Letter From Geraldine to Diane

Dear Diane,

It's been so long since we wrote to each other. Do you remember when we were kids and shared a bedroom, but we still wrote letters anyway? We used to leave them in that dented tin mailbox, and Mr. Howard (the postman, in case you forgot) would deliver them back to the house as if they'd come from the other side of the world. Of course, those letters were more colorful on account of all the crayons we used. These days, we could use a little more of that color.

Ever since Ma and Pa split up, things just haven't been the same. All Ma talks about anymore is her new boyfriend and how he's got some fancy boat he takes her out on. It's so dumb. We obviously aren't going to fall in love with the guy because he's got nice things. But that's Ma. She's always been materialistic and shallow.

Pa isn't happy about it, of course. He's been hitting the bottle harder than usual lately. He's not a nasty drunk, at least, but it seems to bring out some terribly self-destructive tendencies. Sometimes, they come out in full swing, which can be a little scary because it's unpredictable. The other day, for example, he was trying to drive downtown despite being completely drunk as a skunk. I had to hide the keys and take him myself so he wouldn't get behind the wheel and cause an accident. He never used to be this bad. What do you think we should do?

Love,
Geraldine

Letter From Diane to Geraldine

Dear Geraldine,

I've always adored our pen-pal routine, our special little thing. And yes, I do remember Mr. Howard. He used to help me find rare stamps for my stamp collection, at least until I grew older and lost interest in it. He was a kind man.

As for Pa, he's a kind man, too. We both know it. But Ma would paint him as anything but that. In fact, I'm not sure if you're aware of it, but right before they split, Ma started spreading rumors in the church that

Pa had a wicked addiction to pornography and a violent temper. She wove all kinds of unsettling tales about him. None of it was true, of course. I know because I was eavesdropping one day (a piss-poor habit), and I overheard her tell someone on the phone that she had made it all up! The sly devil. Ma actually admitted to driving Pa crazy on purpose so he'd ask for a divorce. That way, she'd have an easier time convincing people that she didn't want one—that it was all him. Those fools and gossip hounds ate it up, to no surprise. They supported her silly nonsense and turned on Pa without so much as asking him once for his side of the story. Not once! That's why he won't go to church anymore. He'd been jaded long before that, but this was the last straw. I can't say I blame him.

Sorry if you're hearing about all this for the first time. If Pa didn't tell you about it, he might only be trying to spare your feelings. He knows how devout you've always been. That aside, we should probably look into options like intervention and maybe even rehab for Pa. We need to address this. It's long overdue.

Yours Truly,
Diane

Letter From Geraldine to Diane

Dear Diane,

Thank you for letting me know what Ma did to our poor father. I always knew she was manipulative, but I had no idea she would stoop to that low a level. Shame on the congregation for being so quick to believe a false truth without questioning it. Though, I can't say I'm overly surprised that Ma would pull a ruse like that. "I write whatever checks I see fit to," she used to say. "It's up to Cody to make sure they can cash em." I'm starting to realize that that was her way of acknowledging the responsibility for her actions would always fall on Pa—and now, thinking back on our childhood, a lot is starting to make sense. She was a gosh-dang conniving ~~bitch~~ (pardon the language) jerk!

Anyway, I agree that we should try arranging an intervention to address Pa's drinking problem before things get out of hand. You and I both know that should he ever actually hurt someone, he'll never forgive himself. If an intervention doesn't work, we will need to get him into rehab somehow. Let me know if you can get the rest of the family together. I'll reach out to some friends of his this week. We can do this, Diane. I know it's not your thing, but please keep it in your prayers.

Love,
Geraldine

Letter From Diane to Geraldine

Dear Geraldine,

You're one silly lady sometimes, you know that? Using a word like "bitch" isn't going to ruin your chances of getting to Heaven—I promise! That said, yes, an intervention is a solid plan of action. I spoke with the family (except for our "jerk" mother, of course), and they all agreed to it. All we need to do now is schedule it and make sure Dad shows up. Let me know how it goes with his friends, and don't stress so much, alright? Dad's going to be ok.

Yours Truly,
Diane

Letter From Geraldine to Diane

Dear Diane,

Dad's friends are on board, but we need to make this happen soon. He got in serious trouble for running a red light. He almost smashed into a minivan with three small children inside! It's only a matter of time before he does something irreversible. We need to act fast, so let's aim to do this next Thursday when he comes over for supper. Tell everyone to park down at the Wells' old place and to arrive an hour early.

He won't like this, but it has to be done. He hasn't
given us much of a choice.

Love,
Geraldine

Cody placed the letters back down on the bar top. He
put his hands over his face as tears streamed along his
bearded cheeks. Faina rubbed her hand over his back
to comfort him. "I remember now," Cody said. "I
remember everything."

"What happened?" asked Rue.

Cody wiped away his tears and let out a long sigh.
"I made some bad choices in my life. One of em, in
particular, was marrying my wife—or ex-wife—Lisa.
The only good thing to come from it was it gave me
four beautiful children. Two of em are my daughters,
Diane and Geraldine. They're the ones who wrote
these letters.

"Throughout my life, I've experienced some
hardships. But that divorce was the hardest damn
thing I ever went through, and I did what I swore I'd

never do. I became my father. I hit the bottle, and the more I consumed, the more of me it consumed in return. I done fucked up my whole life after that. Almost killed a family on the road because of my foolishness. But my daughters? They were just tryin to look out for my sorry ass—and how did I thank em? I ran away."

"Where did you go?"

"The afternoon before my girls planned on holdin that intervention, a friend of mine slipped up—clued me in by accident. Naturally, I wanted no part of it. So, I didn't show up the evening I was supposed to be there. I went to the dock where Lisa's boyfriend's boat was hitched. The dummy left his keys in an unlocked deck box. I took the boat out off the coast a lil ways and drank as much as it took to put this ol boozehound to sleep. I remember wakin up to the sound of a storm outside the cabin, and then I passed out again. Next thing I knew, I was here on the island."

Makoto moved from the table and sat beside Cody. "What I don't understand," he said, "is why this truth is so important. How does it connect you to the island?"

"I ain't sure what it's got to do with the island," Cody answered, "but I reckon I needed to be sober and clear-headed to see this side of me and how it was hurtin my kids. I was selfish. Unwillin to see my wrongs." Cody pushed his untouched glass of whiskey toward Makoto. "At least now I can see how to right em," he said.

"Maybe that's why we're here," Rue replied. "Maybe we were brought here to see a side of ourselves we otherwise couldn't see. Maybe we're so close to our problems that we can't see we are the problem. We're being forced to step back from it all so we can see things for what they are."

Makoto raised his eyebrows in thought. "You're suggesting this place is like a mirror?" he asked.

Rue nodded. "Maybe there's hope for us after all."

"Hope is all we had since we got here," Cody replied. "Now, we're gettin somewhere."

An unnatural snickering erupted at one end of the bar. Perched upon the countertop was the cat. It's back arched. Hackles raised. A baleful grin across its face. Its chortling turned to hysterical laughter, so eldritch and otherworldly that a chill flowed through each survivor.

Why is it doing that? Faina asked, her signing almost frantic. Rue shook her head with uncertainty.

"Shut up, stupid cat!" Dolion shouted. He lurched up in anger and slammed his fist down next to it. The cat hissed and sunk its teeth into Dolion's hand. Straight to the bone. He cried out, and the cat withdrew from its bite. Blood pumped from the punctures and ran down over his fingers and onto the bar. All at once, it seemed as though the walls had begun to undulate, but it was not the walls that were in motion. Innumerable spiders, rat-like in size, crept down along them from wide cracks near the ceiling and surged to the floor. Rue fled from the tavern with the others. As the blood from Dolion's wound trailed behind them, the spiders fed upon the blood. She could hear the cat still laughing at them.

Revolver

The survivors paused to catch their breath. Cold air entered their lungs and escaped through flared nostrils. Raindrops tapped against the exterior of their jackets and rolled down their dirty sleeves. Dolion inspected his bloody hand, and Rue removed from her pocket a shred of cloth a few feet in length that she had saved from her former campsite. She unrolled the cloth and stretched it until the fabric was taut enough to wrap over his wound.

"Wait," Lyssa said. She produced a small flask embroidered with the tavern's logo. "You can use this to clean it."

"You find all the good stuff," Rue replied.

Dolion reached out his hand, and Lyssa poured vodka over the punctures in his skin. When the alcohol entered the wounds, he winced. "Relax, you won't get drunk," Lyssa said facetiously.

Dolion surrendered a slight smile as Rue circled his hand with the cloth, wrapping it in firm layers. "Thanks," he said, "I know I'm the last person either of you want to help right now."

"We're all in this together," Rue replied.

"Of course."

"I've got to say, that was an unusually nasty bite for a house cat."

"I've been bitten by plenty of cats before, but this was worse than any of them. I swear that thing went to the bone."

"Looks deep enough."

"It was strong. Never felt anything like it."

"Well, I've never seen walls come alive with spiders, but here we are. Less and less surprises me the longer we're on the island."

"I agree with you there."

"What do you mean you've been bitten by cats before?" Lyssa asked.

Dolion looked up at her with bemusement. "I don't think I understand the ques—"

"I mean, how do you know you've been bitten by 'plenty of cats' if you can't remember anything about your past?"

Lyssa glared at Dolion, but he looked away, waving her off. "There are other cats on the island," he said condescendingly. "I ran into them lots of times. This is just the worst of the bites, that's all."

Rue and Lyssa exchanged distrusting glances but had little else to say.

After treating Dolion's wound, the group pressed on. They headed toward a cluster of nearby buildings and crossed through the neighboring backlot. When they passed over the road, they discovered a schoolhouse.

The school's broad doors were wide open. Inside were numerous desks, miniature in scale. Before each were set chairs. Ropes draped downward from the backs and sagged over the seats. The remnants of pooled blood, the color of charcoaled auburn, lay crusted upon the desks and floor like ancient magma volcanically disgorged over flat earth. Slatherings of the desiccated gore arced from each one toward the center of the classroom and continued out the rear door. A blackboard covered one wall almost in its entirety. Scrawled across it was a phrase in primeval Latin that none of the survivors knew, yet all felt timorous at the sight of it. Childlike whispers seemed to whisk past their ears on the faint cross-breeze that drifted through the building.

When the group stepped out the back door into the schoolyard, they gasped all at once. Infinitesimal shoes and clothing lay in a ceremonious pile next to an ornamented stone oven. An obelisk-like structure towered over the yard and attached to the front, like some sardonic scarecrow, hung a skeleton a third the size of Rue. A mere glance upon this terrible vestige of brutality brought tears to Faina's eyes. Cody looked away in disgust. No one spoke.

The survivors continued walking, examining all that they encountered. They took with them the things they found most useful. There was an apothecary. They meandered about it and browsed its dusty shelves and the wares that lined them. There were handmade candles with decorative labels and medicines kept in ancient jars. The jars had been aged and ambered over time. Bundles of herbs and flowers were tied together with strings and wrapped in thinly woven fabrics. Each of the survivors, in their own way, imagined living in such a time as that which relied on potions and superstition, but Lyssa was bewitched by its antiquated charm far more than the others.

There was a peculiar old stable along the path of exploration. It was blanketed with thick webs, and the delicate, falling rain collected atop them like diamonds bestrewn across a white velour. Over the closed double doors of the stable, there set a large hole. Webs funneled up toward it from the front grounds. Rue thought she saw some dreadful creature scurry past the dark opening, and a shiver ran through her body. *Thank God no one's truth is in there,* she thought.

The survivors came upon a section of road with several houses along both sides. Makoto stopped and looked at one side and then at the other. He seemed, to Rue, to feel some instinct drawing him further in. A moment later, he came at last to the house with the black door. It was locked. Makoto checked the home's perimeter, hoping he might find another way inside. There was no other way. Only a plank of wood, placed between an upstairs window and a window on the neighboring house. Makoto checked to see if the front door to the adjacent house would open, and he was relieved to find that it did. He opened the door. It was too dark to see. Rue withdrew the flashlight from her pocket and pushed the switch with her thumb and pointed it inside.

A white beam of light shone from the flashlight and passed over vintage sofas. The cushions were torn from overuse, and a maple dining table was piled with empty boxes. The spotlight splashed against the peeling walls as roaches fled into the deeper shadows. Makoto followed Rue inside, and the others stayed behind them. They walked up a narrow wooden staircase. The boards beneath their feet creaked with each careful step. When they reached the top, a dark figure was crouched in the corner of the landing. Rue swung the flashlight's beam toward it as the paralysis of fear began to grip her. What she had thought to be some monster lurking there, waiting to pounce, was instead a corpse. It sat slumped in a chair with a portion of its skull opened from the inside out. Next to it lay a revolver containing five .38 caliber bullets, still anticipating the next turn of the cylinder. Makoto picked up the revolver and switched the safety back on and placed the gun into the rear of his belt. He nodded reassuringly to the group.

The survivors checked the rooms on the upper floor until Faina came across the window Makoto had seen from below. One by one, each survivor passed over the plank extended between the houses. Makoto was the first to cross to the other side. He stepped down from the window sill into a bedroom. It was filled with children's toys. Across from the bedroom, on the other side of a narrow stairwell, was the master bedroom. A faded comforter covered a messy bed in the middle of the room. A floral pattern was stitched into the fabric. The threads loosed over time. On top of it, there lay a recording device amidst a pile of bloodied yen.

"This is my truth," Makoto said, "I can feel it."

"Whatever's on that thing," replied Cody, "we're here for you, son."

Makoto nodded and took a deep breath. The survivors gathered around. He sat on the bed, and Rue sat beside him.

Faina formed a heart with her thumbs and index fingers, smiling gently to show her support. Makoto pressed the play button on the recording device.

For My Beloved Kaori

(A Voice Recording)

Translated From Japanese

"Kaori, I don't have much time. I'm dying, and they're coming for me. I don't want to leave you without explaining why I acted dishonorably, so please listen to this recording and not what you see on the news. I need you to understand.

"When I met you, it was the greatest thing that ever happened to me. It brought me so much happiness and joy. The birth of our son, Riku, gave me purpose. You've filled my life with love so great that sometimes I can barely contain how it makes me feel—in case it wasn't evident from how I smothered each of you with affection. It's because of this love that I did what I did.

"A man came by the store a few months ago. He offered me what he called 'an investment opportunity,' but it wasn't an opportunity at all—at least not for me. He was another Yakuza thug wanting to exploit our store. It was only a tiny percentage at first. I didn't want to worry you, so I didn't say anything. After all, that's life in this part of Tokyo. But soon, he took more and then more again. Always more. When the store fell on hard times, I had to take money from its savings. And eventually, our personal savings. I lost the business, Kaori.

"This man took everything from us. He stole everything. And like a coward, I couldn't bring myself to tell you. I knew it would break your heart. So, determined to rebuild our savings, I applied for jobs all over the city. But every company I applied for paid very little, while their management drove around in fancy cars and ate at expensive restaurants. That's when I got angry. A terrible idea took hold of my mind. I would take their money like ours was taken from us.

"I devised a plan. I thought it was the perfect bank robbery. And this morning, when the time was right, I made my move. I executed my plan with every bit of the precision required to be successful. Yet, I still overlooked a crucial detail. An additional security guard was hired who began working today, and because I was unaware, I hadn't accounted for him. This slight oversight was the single thread that unraveled not only my plan but my whole life.

"I did get away with some of the money, but I was wounded in the process. I don't know how much time I have left. Take this money and hide it somewhere— somewhere other than the house. Keep it safe until you can start a new life. I'm a foolish man, and I hope you can find it in your heart to forgive me. Please give my love to Riku, and don't tell him that his father died as a thief. The loss of a father is hard enough on a young boy, never mind one who failed so shamefully. I'm sorry, Kaori. I love you."

Makoto stopped the recording and stared at the floor without a word. "Are you okay?" Rue asked. "I don't think we understood what he said on the recording."

"I killed that man," Makoto said. "My selfish actions killed him." He looked up at Rue. His voice trembled. "I destroyed an entire family!" He cried out, fighting back tears. "Great, he's a murderer," Dolion muttered, "and now he's a murderer with a gun."

"Shut the fuck up," Lyssa said.

"Watch your mouth."

"You watch your mouth, you insensitive jackass," Cody replied. "Let the man have a moment to process without you judgin him."

"I trust Makoto with a gun far more than I trust you with one," added Rue. "You're the cockiest son of bitch here."

Dolion snapped back. "I'm no killer. I'm a good man. A godly man. I would nev—"

"You ain't a man, never mind one of God," Cody said.

"Oh please. You don't know a thing about God."

A menacing cackle echoed from the lower level of the house. Everyone hushed. Downstairs in the dark, the black cat had returned. It emitted the same uncanny laughter as it did in the tavern. The laughter grew in malice as if it were empowered by the arguing survivors. Rue shined the flashlight down the stairwell and saw the cat sitting at the bottom. It grinned and flicked its tail. Another wave of light flooded the room behind it, and Rue realized the front door had opened. In came an apparition like those she encountered in the forest. It floated across the floor to the bottom of the stairwell and looked up at her. Its face was an elk skull, and strands of flesh hung from its antlers. The vile, drooling hounds crept in too, and they gathered around it.

Rue screamed, and the survivors rallied behind her. They panicked when they saw the demonic assembly at the bottom of the stairwell. The survivors bolted back towards the open window through which they came, and once more, they darted across the plank one by one. Dolion and Faina were the last to attempt the crossing. As the feral dogs stampeded up the stairs, shouldering each other against the walls and banister, their howling and snapping jaws drew nearer. Faina tried to pull herself through the window, but Dolion lurched past her. She slipped and fell between the houses.

"Faina!" Rue shrieked as the hounds filled the room on the other side. Lyssa ran down to the road with the others following closely on her heels. Faina was limping away from the space between the houses, struggling to keep on her feet. Lyssa threw her head beneath Faina's right arm and pulled it around the back of her neck to support her weight, and Makoto did the same on her left side. There was a brick building at the end of the road with a solid steel door. They thought it might offer protection. The survivors raced for the door, knowing their lives depended on it. Lyssa looked down at Faina's leg. She saw it was broken and hanging loose below the knee. The dogs tore out of the house, barking and yowling like banshees, clawing at the earth as they tried to catch their prey.

Rue was the first to reach the steel door. *Please let it be unlocked,* she thought. She slammed the handle down and pulled it toward her. The door swung open with a metallic creak. She held it, waving the others in. Cody and Dolion ran inside. Straggling behind in the road, Makoto and Lyssa dragged Faina as fast as they could, but the dogs caught up to them. One bit fiercely into Faina's leg, knocking all three survivors to the ground. Faina squealed in pain. A hound hooked Lyssa's sleeve with its sharp teeth, and Makoto pulled the gun from his belt and fired a blind shot at the dog. The bullet passed through its eye, and it yelped and let go. Faina screamed in terror as the dogs snapped at her from every direction.

"Get inside!" Makoto shouted at Lyssa. She bolted through the open door as Makoto aimed his gun. He fired three more shots into the pack. They had little effect on the wretched beasts, and he threw the gun to the ground. He kicked and punched at them in desperation, but there was nothing more he could do. A force beyond his understanding drove the animals, and to the horror of the survivors, Faina pleaded and shrieked and wailed in agony as she was torn apart by the hounds.

Samaritan

Lyssa slammed shut the door behind Makoto. She gasped for breath as she slid the lock bolt into place. The remaining survivors stood inside a storage room as Makoto shook his head. He gestured distressingly toward the door where Faina was left to die on the other side. "I couldn't save her," he said. "I tried, but they wouldn't stop!"

"That's not on you," Lyssa said reassuringly.

"It isn't on anyone," Dolion replied.

"No, it's on you, you miserable bastard!" Rue shouted. She lunged at Dolion, beating at his chest with all her might. Dolion put up his arms to shield himself. She kept swinging until Cody pulled her away. "You're the reason she's dead!" Rue continued. "She fell because you pushed her through that window, you fucking coward!" Everyone looked at Dolion.

"Is this true?" asked Makoto.

"Of course not," Dolion replied.

"Oh shut the fuck up," Lyssa said sneeringly, "you two-faced lose—"

Dolion slapped her across the face. The others were stunned, but before they could react, Lyssa grinned, tasting her blood in her mouth. She hit him back, raking her pointed nails across his face.

"It's true—I saw it," Lyssa said. "Why do you think I was the first one running down to help her?"

"That's bullshit," Dolion replied. He rubbed his scratched cheek. Something caught Lyssa's eye, and she noticed a folded piece of paper lying on the ground; it had fallen from Dolion's pocket when she slapped him. She reached down to pick it up.

"No, wait!" he shouted, attempting to snatch it from her.

Lyssa drew her knife, and Dolion leaped back. "What's this?" she asked. She unfolded the paper.

Disgraced Pastor Ousted From Church

(A Newspaper Clipping)

Today, fresh allegations against a well-known megachurch pastor have surfaced, forcing an ousting that many in Evergreen County say is long overdue. They bring to light some of the glaring problems critics of the church have pointed out for decades, ranging from severe hypocrisy to abuse from leadership.

In recent years, Crusades Of The Heart Church has been known for rallying followers against a wide range of social reforms. For example, last year, it led a march against gay marriage despite the protective legislature already being passed. Yet the pastor is accused of having sexual and adulterous relationships with several male church members. When one of these members, James Dawson, begged him to come forward, the beloved pastor rejected a public confession. Instead, he offered money from church funding to buy Dawson's silence.

"He wanted me to come to his house and spend the night while his wife was out," Dawson said, "but I told him no. I was just like—I can't keep doing this [sneaking around]. I wanted to come out—come clean, you know? That's when Pastor Dolion offered to give me money in exchange for keeping my mouth shut. I didn't feel right about it, so I told somebody."

In addition to sexual misconduct, there are numerous accounts of other forms of harassment and abuse from leadership. However, the primary reason for the ousting is allegedly due to reports that investigators have gathered evidence of embezzlement and fraudulent behavior. Representatives for Pastor Dolion did not respond to our calls or requests for comment.

Lyssa read the newspaper clipping, then passed it to the others. Dolion nervously watched them from across the room. "You been sittin on this the whole time?" Cody asked. Dolion stayed silent.

"He said he never met Riel," recalled Rue. "Now we know he was lying from the start."

"Of course he lied," Lyssa replied. "This prick doesn't want us to know who or what he is. He wants us to think he's some saint—which, literal news flash, he's not."

Makoto held up the newspaper clipping. "When did you get this, Dolion?" he asked.

"Before I found you people," Dolion answered.

"Before he found us," Cody muttered in a rankled tone. "That ain't how I remember it."

"Say what you will," Dolion said defensively. "I never said I was perfect. But as a Christian, at least I'm forgiven. You say you're a Christian, Cody, but you're not. You're one in name only, or else you wouldn't act the way you do. You're an alcoholic and use foul language. You protect secular deviants over your own kind. Maybe if all of you cared more about your souls, we'd all be off this forsaken island already."

"That's a good one, Dolion," replied Cody. He sat down on an empty crate and leaned forward. "Let me do you one better. Once upon a time, Jesus was speakin to His followers, as He often did. Some guy in the crowd asks how a person gains eternal life. Jesus lays it out real simple—believe in God and love your neighbor as yourself. The man, with what I can only assume is a dumb look on his face, tries Jesus again. 'Yeah, but define neighbor,' he says.

"Jesus looks at him and tells his people the story of the good Samaritan. Tells em about a guy who's been beaten and robbed and left for dead on the side of a road, only to be passed by and spat on by a supposedly spiritual man. Then comes another—the Samaritan, who don't judge. He just sees a guy in need and saves his life without question and without expecting anything in return. Even pays for his recovery. So what about you, Dolion? You been helpin people or pushin em from windows?"

"How dare you," said Dolion sneeringly. "How dare you try to twist God's Word against me. You don't know a thing about God's law!"

"I know that humans can barely interpret their own laws. I'm not so sure I trust how well they interpret the Almighty's."

"Alright, enough," Makoto said. He turned toward Dolion. "Dolion, it's time for you to part ways with the rest of us."

"What are you saying?" Dolion asked.

"I'm saying you're on your own."

"You can't do that to me. I'll die out there!"

"I'm sorry, but you'll have to take your chances. If we keep you with us, we're taking ours by having you around."

"What's that supposed to mean?"

Lyssa furrowed her brow. "It means that everyone already sleeps with one eye open," she said, "and if we need to sleep with the other one open, we might as well not sleep at all."

Dolion's panic grew as he looked at each survivor. "Please, you can trust me," he insisted. "I swear—I'm not who you think I am!"

"You've done nothing but talk down to us for not believing the same things as you," Rue said sternly. "You lied to us about already knowing your past, you assaulted my friend, and you got poor Faina killed. I'd say you're exactly who we think you are."

Dolion shook his head. Unbeknownst to him, Rue did not wish to send forth a companion alone into peril, but she knew all the same that a man who would not concede his wrongdoings could not be trusted to protect anyone but himself. "You're all insane," Dolion said. "You're casting me out, yet you're following the orders of that demon Riel? Do you honestly believe he's on your side? He strips us of our memories and taunts us by rubbing our noses in our mistakes, then uses the promise of answers to lure us to our deaths. In fact, I'll bet you this one is in on it!" Dolion pointed at Lyssa. "I bet they sent her to join our group. They wanted her to spy on us and divide us. Why else did that cat buddy up to her back at the tavern before it attacked us?"

Rue noticed Lyssa seemed taken aback by the insinuation and found her silence unusual, given her tendency for a snappy retort. "Yeah, she knows what I'm talking about," Dolion continued. "She's got all this hate and darkness in her. Surely, you all see how she always seems right at home on the island. She practically lusts after it. She's the only one unphased by anything we come across, so long as she's not herself in any danger. You think it's me you can't trust, but you'll see. You just wait."

"We're leaving now," Makoto said to Dolion. "I suggest you don't hang around here too long. They'll come searching sooner or later."

"You can't stop me from coming with you, and you know it."

"You already got slapped in the face. Are you really looking to see what getting punched feels like?"

"You wouldn—"

"Try me."

"Fine," Dolion said defeatedly, "I'll go."

"Thank you."

"I guess you're just a thug after all."

Makoto glared at Dolion but said nothing. The survivors continued to the front of the building and went out into the gloom, leaving Dolion behind. It was getting darker. As they walked, they watched like sentinels for a place to spend the night.

The shopfronts and houses sprawled further from one another. On the horizon loomed the immense silhouette of a castle-like structure.

"I ain't sure I like the looks of that," said Cody.

"It might be the asylum," Rue replied.

"Then I definitely don't like the looks of it."

"That's where Lyssa's truth is."

Lyssa shook her head. "Let's just figure out where to rest," she said. "We can worry about that tomorrow."

"I'm not sure where to go next," said Makoto.

"There's a couple more houses over there," Cody replied. "Maybe we can hole up in one of em. Cross our fingers and hope them monsters keep the hell out for the night."

"We've had enough hell, thank you very much," Rue said humorously.

Makoto looked around at the nearby houses. "Which one should we try?" he asked.

Riel's voice whispered suddenly in Rue's ear, and she pointed toward a house. It had closed shutters. One was broken and hung by a single hinge. The outer walls were covered by vines that crept up and wrapped themselves around the panes and the chimney like greedy serpents, disseminating in some vain attempt to consume the world.

"Are you sure?" Makoto asked.

"I'm sure."

The survivors entered the house. Night had fallen, and they discussed which room was safest to sleep in. There was an old stove. Wood logs lay waiting beside it. They would have made a fire by which to keep warm had it not been for the plume of smoke that would be visible against the pale face of the moon. Against a wall, there leaned a bookcase containing an assortment of fine literature. Decorative trinkets were set upon the shelves. Rue curiously inspected each object while the others settled. As she held in her hand a rough, whittled carving, Riel's voice whispered again. "Someone help me move this bookcase," Rue said.

Cody and Makoto grabbed the bookcase and slid it aside. It revealed a small opening. Behind the space was a staircase leading down into a dark cellar. Cody took a step back and stroked his beard. "Well, I'll be damned," he said.

"How did you know?" asked Makoto.

"Riel," Rue replied. "When we were outside, his voice spoke to me. He pointed me to this house. After we came inside, the bookcase caught my eye. He said to move it but didn't say what we'd find."

"I can't say I like it."

"Me neither," Cody added.

Makoto looked at Rue. "What do you want to do?" he asked.

Rue shrugged. "I don't think any of us want to sleep in this house knowing there might be a mysterious murder tomb lurking under it," she said.

"She's got a point," replied Cody.

Rue shined the flashlight into the cellar and stepped forward, but Makoto stopped her. "Let me," he said. "I'll go first."

"Are you sure?"

"I'm sure."

Rue handed Makoto the flashlight, and she followed behind him and Cody and Lyssa behind her. As they descended the cellar stairs, they looked closely at the walls. What seemed like a hundred crucifixes hung on each side. All different sizes. Scriptural passages had been scrawled in the spaces between them. At the bottom of the stairwell, Makoto reached a closed door. It's edges stuck to the frame, and he wiggled it loose and opened it. A musty smell swept upward through the corridor. He shined the flashlight into a pitch-black room.

In the room was a desk piled with books and stationery items. A typewriter was draped in cobwebs, its keys and mechanisms speckled with corrosion. In the corner was a bed. Beneath the covers lay a skeleton leaning to one side. On a nightstand next to the bed sat an oil lantern. Lyssa ignited it. In the warm glow of the lantern, the cellar illuminated. The group examined a myriad of curiosities strewn about. There were carved statues and ancient-looking relics. Personal belongings that were part of stories they would never know.

Rue studied the skeleton curiously. "What killed this one if they were so well hidden?" she asked.

"I reckon they might've died naturally," Cody replied. "They're tucked neatly in the bed, and there ain't no weapons or pills around."

"No blood, either," added Lyssa.

Cody glanced around the room. "Looks like they been livin down here a long time before passin away."

"I wonder if they were on the island before it got like this," Rue considered aloud, "or if they came here afterward like we did."

Makoto shrugged as he thumbed through documents stacked on the cluttered desk. "I think you're going to want to see this," he said.

Incarnate

Professor Amani's Memorandum

To you who've stumbled upon these writings, it's either by pure luck or divine guidance that you should walk into someone's house and feel the urge to push aside a bookcase to see what fascinations may lie in wait behind it. After all, who doesn't go traipsing through strangers' homes, sliding their furniture about in hopes that such spontaneous rearrangements might lead to some spectacularly splendid discovery? Not me, of course. But I enjoy imagining the sort of fellow who might someday find my secret hypogean hideaway.

If you're here reading these words, then I can only assume this to be one of only a few distinct scenarios: one where this awful island is still quite awful, or perhaps one where it's not and has since received a shiny new lease on life; where you're here to renovate this former abode and transform it into something a little less dank and a whole lot less sinister. Unfortunately, the former of these possibilities is likely your reality. I offer my condolences, dear friend. But do not fret—you're in luck! I've gathered information about this place, which may prove insightful to you.

When I woke up on the isle, my memory was debilitated. It failed me in ways I didn't understand. My first consideration was amnesia, yet no sign of trauma was visible—no injury to my head. Thus, there were no reasons I could think of for such symptomatology. This was troubling, of course, but I could do little to remedy it. So, I set out to find help.

After a brief period of wandering, I found this village. It didn't take long for me to see that something about it was unusual. Peculiar sightings and ghastly encounters plagued every attempt I made to escape. There was nothing I could do but wait for some rescue party that would never arrive. If ever I found myself in the company of another, they were gone posthaste—either no longer heard from in their pursuit of personal objectives or lost to gruesome ends.

One particularly fateful night, a man by the name of Riel woke me from sleep. After a short and less-than-satisfactory conversation, he gave me an assignment: to visit a place where I would find answers. I'm not a fool, so naturally, I was suspicious. But I had nothing better to do, and it gave me purpose and a sense of possibility. My memory loss, the dull ache of loneliness, and the terrors lurking beyond every corner made living more daunting than dying. Having a new direction gave me hope, so I sought to find the truth meant for me to discover.

Reaching my destination was an arduous task. When I arrived, the location turned out to be a modestly sized library. It was packed to the ceiling with books. A plethora of them overflowed from the shelves. There was a little reading nook meant for a child, and I found a series of drawings tucked inside it. They were crudely adolescent and meaningless to any who might see them, but they meant something to me. All at once, my memories were restored. A wave of emotions flooded my very soul, something I didn't believe I possessed until that moment. I saw my life in a new light. More importantly, I could see the mistakes that led me to this place with greater clarity. I finally knew how to return to my former life and correct the path on which I'd traveled with reckless abandon.

The return of my memory meant knowing both my present self and my past self. I remembered everything, including my career as a professor of history at a prestigious university. With my rediscovered affinity for the past came a genuine curiosity regarding the isle's origin. How was it discovered, and where is it located? When was the village established? What makes the weather so consistently dismal, without so much as a speck of sunlight for countless days? And most importantly, how did such wickedness come to roam the landscape?

I waited patiently for another visit from the mystic, Riel. However, interest in the isle's past grew into an obsession that begged to be satiated, lest the unanswered questions drive me into madness.

When Riel finally appeared to me, he gave me my last order. He pointed me to where I could escape the island and return home. I rejected this opportunity. A surprise, even to myself. My need to understand what happened here was too great. So I stayed. I stayed and began collecting every clue I could find. Now, my dear fellow, I present to you these findings.

Letter From Benjamin Baker To Dr. Nathaniel Radison

Dr. Radison,

Salem has changed significantly since the trials ended little more than a century ago. As you might have guessed, these changes are not all for the best. This is because the witchcraft that plagued that town is still alive and well, for how could it simply disappear without protections in place to identify and eradicate it? The state, however, is not turning a blind eye to this problem. Condoning of evil shall not be tolerated. Yet we must accept that many will stand against us should we openly persecute those espousing devious ideologies and devilish practices. Ignorance and naivety are bountiful, as you know. That is why the state has decided to acquire an uninhabited isle near the coast to relocate those engaged in witchcraft and other unrighteous behavior. We are determined to reduce their evil influences on our citizenry.

The state is building an institution to assist in rehabilitating any witches and undesirables we send there. We will establish housing for caretakers as well. This is where you are best able to serve us: we want you to lead the effort by taking residence on the isle and overseeing the construction of facilities, along with managing all functions thereafter. Most importantly, once routines are in order, you must ensure no one leaves the isle without state approval. Any outgoing letters or parcels that might draw unwanted contention from our guests' loved ones should also be diverted for the good of all. We do not want to reintroduce any heretics to society before we have adequately corrected their ideals and behaviors.

Should you accept our request for your assistance, please know that we will handsomely reward your efforts and provide you with daily provisions and suitable lodging. Please consider our offer and let us know if you accept. Preferably within the fortnight, lest we find another candidate before then.

Sincerely,
Benjamin Baker

Letter From Dr. Nathaniel Radison To Benjamin Baker

Mr. Baker,

The institution is finally complete and running as planned. The first of our guests arrived Thursday morning. They have been cooperative thus far. Not surprisingly, a few have been less than pleased with their situation and have challenged the basis of their stay here. Rest assured, though, all is well. I will be in touch regarding their rehabilitation and, with any luck, return them to their families soon. We shall celebrate and discuss future opportunities upon my next visit to the capital! Until then, best of luck in the upcoming election.

Cordially,
Dr. Nathaniel Radison

Letter From Benjamin Baker
To Dr. Nathaniel Radison

Dr. Radison,

It has been quite some time since the first delivery of guests reached the isle. Though there have been unfortunate setbacks, we believe the endeavor has been a success overall. Some of the caretakers have noticed you have been partaking in the spirits much these days, so we want to take a moment to express our sincerest appreciation for your incredible work. We will add our finest brandy to the next shipment of provisions sent to the isle.

Nathaniel, I can not insist enough: you are not to blame for any heretics who fail in their rehabilitation.

If they choose to leap from windows or cast themselves off cliffs or drown while attempting to swim to the mainland, then so be it. These lost sheep should be grateful for our shepherding and not guilt us with tantrums and self-harm. They only see their visit as captivity, but it is not captivity. It is salvation.

I should mention that there has been a peculiar increase in unsavory characters and uncivilized vagabonds harassing townsfolk in nearby settlements. We intend to gather as many of them as possible and send them to the isle. It is better for our people that these troublemakers stay off roads and out of taverns and inns. We want them out of sight entirely.

Once they are on the isle, you will have full custody as always. With no one to identify this particular lot, you shall have plenty of suitable candidates for your next set of experiments. Just make sure what happens at the institution is not spoken of elsewhere, do you understand? Ensure your staff knows the consequences, lest they find themselves unforgivably garrulous the next time they come to the mainland. If you require anything, do write, for we will fulfill any needs expeditiously.

Sincerely,
Benjamin Baker

Letter From Dr. Nathaniel Radison To Benjamin Baker

Mr. Baker,

I received your most recent inquiry regarding the arrival of our new guests. Yes, it's true; many arrived with pleasant attitudes. They were satisfied to have a hot meal and a place to rest their heads, unexposed to the harsh brutality of the elements. Autumn is upon us, after all, and the nights will only grow colder.

There was, however, a man among them by the name of Theodore Kingsley. He has been rousing some of the guests. Our guards have had to separate him from the others on numerous occasions. For example, he was caught fornicating with several women accused of witchcraft. He even attempted to perform some dark ritual with them. Lord knows what they tried to conjure. At times, he lashes out in violence, attacking anyone in sight. Even his friends. Despite his aggressive behavior, he has an intoxicating effect on them, for they follow his lead regardless of the abuse he directs toward them.

Two nights ago, Theodore was accused of having raped one of our caretakers—a gentle soul who has been with us from the beginning. She said Kingsly entered her room as she slept, and she awoke with his hand over her mouth, her bedroom door locked shut. There was little she could do, for her fright was too great. She had not the power to resist him. He carved a strange shape into her inner thigh, like a brand you might see on cattle. That poor girl.

Last night, we placed Theodore in one of the rooms where I conduct my experiments. We chained him to the wall and attempted an interrogation. He spat upon us. He thrashed about, screaming and retching with the strangest delight. When he refused to answer my questions, I inflicted pain upon him. That only seemed to intensify his wild behavior. His vile cachinnation.

Something quite unsettling happened after that. I referred to Kingsley by his first name, Theodore, as we always have. He said this was not his real name. I pressed him, for we all wished to know what he meant. Had he been lying to us the whole time? He remained silent. I shouted angrily at him, demanding that he answer me. There was another long pause that felt like an eternity, and then he looked at me with a twisted expression that contorted his face. "I am Incarnate," he said. I told him to explain himself. "You know," he said. "You know." At this point, Kingsley continued to scream and laugh and thrash about.

To make matters worse, isolating Theodore in confinement seems to have agitated his followers. This morning, there is an alarming state of vitriol in their sentiment toward our staff. Some are acting out in ways far more disturbing than usual. We fear that if we do not find a way to quell this unrest, things may escalate beyond what we are able to control, for we are only ever prepared to subdue a few offenders at one time—not suppress a mutiny. We will be in your debt if you can send trained men to assist the guards. Please advise, and we shall handle things accordingly.

Cordially,
Nathaniel Radison

Father Abraham's Journal

April 27th.

What a beautiful day. The sun is shining, and the birds sing in such melodies that you can close your eyes and lose yourself in reverie. As I write this, I await the boat that will take me to my new home on Raven Island. Some superstitious townsfolk in nearby Salem believe it to be cursed. It is one of the reasons I was asked to lead the church there.

Over the past few years, they have worked diligently to restore the old institution and build new dwellings and stores. They are even constructing a kind of metal tower they say will aid in bringing electricity to the isle. These are wonderful improvements. What was once a blasphemous exercise in human indecency has now been given a chance to move on in a positive way. Alas, a tragedy befell the isle in its earlier days. But with the help of the good Lord and perhaps a little luck, we might have a chance to set things right—so long as the people want it too, of course.

Many years ago, this island was a place forged in the name of God, yet it was anything but Christ-like. Before that were the notorious witch trials of Salem. The trials were baseless, and many innocents perished in terrible ways. Even a mere child was put to death; bless her soul! The thought of it always brings sadness to my heart. And what was it all for? Fear of sin and sorcery caused families and neighbors to turn on one another without so much as a benefit of the doubt. They were pressured into false admissions for which they were punished regardless.

When it was thought to be over, it was not. The allegations continued, and those accused were whisked away in secret to Raven Island. There, they were institutionalized and forced into religious and ideological compliance. Those who resisted most were tortured and experimented upon. All it took was one insane devil of a human to win the hearts of the secular captives and ignite a deadly insurrection. Nathaniel Radison, that wolf in sheep's clothing, was burned at the stake by a lunatic and his followers. Oh, the irony.

More tragic is that the bloodshed did not end there. Soldiers were sent to the island, and all the inmates, or "guests," as Radison liked to call them, were killed on site. Though one might be tempted to assume they all deserved this fate, it's important to consider that many of these individuals were taken from their homes. An insinuation of religious deviancy was all it took for them to be forcibly separated from their families. Vengeance is not moral and rarely justice, but it is human nonetheless. Sometimes, it deserves at least the courtesy of one's empathy.

Oh my, look at the time! That is enough history for today. The boat is approaching, and there is much for me to think about. I am to evaluate the community and determine how best to serve it.

July 20th.

Oh, how I loathe the summer heat. Though, I do enjoy watching the people of this town indulge in it. Young couples taking walks along the shoreline. Children laughing and skipping about. There is much in the way of fishing here, and I have greatly enjoyed some rather delectable spreads of fresh fish. The sun also sets later, of course, so there are many evenings I get to sit and take in the beauty that God hath put forth for us to marvel at through wide eyes.

Sunday services have been busy since my arrival, though they seem to be thinning lately. It sometimes happens, for it is not uncommon to see a pendulum-like repetition in congregations. When life is good, they drift away. When times are hard, they return with greater consistency. Overall, I am happy with how things have turned out here. Seeing the town grow and evolve in such a short time has been a blessing, and I am grateful to be a part of it.

August 9th,

I watched the isle's first automotive vehicle arrive today. While I sat, I met a strange young couple: the Moores. The husband was a handsome fellow, and his wife a natural beauty. They were nothing but friendly and warm toward Sister Nancy and me. Yet we each found something odd about the couple's demeanor. Their presence gave off a sort of startling energy I could not put my finger on. That aside, I enjoyed chatting with them as we all took in the delightful summer weather. Mr. Moore said they have lived on the island since its revival. I do not recall having ever seen them before. Perhaps these old eyes need checking!

On another note, Mrs. McCleary came to me today and asked if we could pray, she and I. She was worried for her beloved cat, Jester. He has not been seen in days. The feline is ever the rascal, as many are—climbing through the neighbors' windows and causing all kinds of mischief and hilarity. Hopefully, he is simply partaking in a lengthy romp and is not lying ill beneath a house somewhere. Either way, we prayed for Jester.

September 12th.

All is not well. The congregation is dwindling. Jester's whereabouts are still unknown. Worse, a child has gone missing! The Bernstein family's youngest son, Timothy, went into the woods on Tuesday and never came home. Mr. Moore has been leading searches across the isle to locate Timothy while I hold vigils at the church. Sister Nancy tries to console the poor boy's mother and attends to her as needed. My heart breaks for her. It hurts for this community.

September 28th.

A murder has taken place on the island—a terrible, horrible murder. Mr. Norwich, an elderly gentleman like myself, was found tied between timber. His throat was cut. His skull crushed. There was a pattern of lacerations along the forearms. The unsettling placement of demonic symbols and effigies set about the site adds more consternation to an already reprehensible slaying. It was not murder for greed nor lust or vengeance; this was encouraged by some great evil. No, not only encouraged—done in the name of evil itself, for evil is still alive and well here.

Oh, what dread! I came to this place hoping to heal it from the evils falsely enacted in God's name. I have already failed. Tonight, for the first time, we will lock the doors of our homes while we sleep.

October 7th.

Someone has painted the same devilish symbols from Mr. Norwich's murder in blood throughout the village. More dismaying is that the Moores have been holding clandestine meetings at odd hours of the night. On more than one occasion, I awoke in the night. I could see my neighbors sneaking away in the direction of the woods. I fear what they may be doing there and suspect that unholy practices are at play. I do not know what to do. Confronting this directly may cost me my life, yet if I do nothing, it may cost others theirs. In the morning, I will send a message to the mainland and request that the authorities aid us with a formal investigation. This has gone far beyond the abilities of an old priest.

October 14th.

There is no reaching the mainland. I have attempted to send letters, but it has become apparent that those delivering them are destroying them instead. Worse, when I try leaving the isle, I am told that our perfectly capable vessels are unusable. There is no way off other than to swim in the chilly waters when the waves are at their calmest. Sadly, at my age, I am not confident in my ability to last the entirety of the crossing. I am stranded here, and they are planning something. I do not know what, but I am fraught with terror at the thought of what it might be.

October 31st.

I am in a living nightmare, and the horrors of Hell hath overtaken the isle. The Moores have not only conjured great evils—they are evil incarnate. The couple forged a sinister cult, turning the townspeople to their cause one by one. Those of us who resist are outnumbered, and tonight, we are being hunted. I can hear the screams of the innocent on the roads. Women and children are being raped and tortured. Husbands and fathers are bound and forced to watch before they too, are mutilated. All are eventually sacrificed to pagan deities and ancient devils.

The moon is full. Clouds crawl past them while the repulsive aroma of wet blood and burning flesh perfuses the air. Sister Nancy and I are sick with dread and hold close to one another, hiding in the study as the cornered prey we have been reduced to. There is chanting that grows with vehemence beyond the walls of the church. We are surrounded.

They are trying to break down the doors to the sanctuary, hacking at them with dense clubs and bladed weapons. The stained glass windows are being shattered by thrown rocks. They are pelting them like hail. As I spy the sanctuary from the hall, I can see the hot glow of fires and billowing black smoke. They are trying to burn down the church. They aim to kill us.

Minutes pass, yet their flames do not seem to take. A voice outside says the outer walls will not burn. Another offers a bottle of rye and cloth, and someone ignites the fabric, which is tucked inside the container of alcohol. They throw it through a window, but the flame is snuffed out as the bottle tumbles across the floor. I do not know what keeps them at bay, but perhaps something spiritual works in our favor.

The horde is leaving for now; I suspect they will return. Sister Nancy and I will rest while we can. We know not what is yet to come.

November 4th.

Five days of brutality. Five days of slaughter. People I once called friends, brothers, and sisters are either the slayers or the slain. I am alone, for even Sister Nancy has taken her life to escape what cruel torture might have otherwise befell her.

I keep asking myself why—why is this terrible thing happening? My thoughts on this go around and around for countless hours, day by day. My conclusion is always the same: the isle was doomed from the beginning. As I have pointed out before, the foundation for Raven Island's community was built on injustices done in the name of our Lord without the Lord's consent. Through open doors of resentment and hate, a great evil attached itself to these indignities and spread like some malignant disease in the hearts of those persecuted. Upon their deaths, these poor souls were buried in the ground like seeds, and from these seeds, the ethos of the Enemy Of God hath germinated, strangling any good that may come here.

Alas, a man who suffers under the woes of persecution eventually rebels. When his judgments are thrust upon him by religion, is it not then that he will seek the opposite of the thing? Evil men who masquerade as good men deliver good men to evil, and while darkness is the absence of light, light may sometimes be the mask that darkness wears to conceal itself. Thus, light begins to look like darkness, and darkness appears as light. As above, so below. Perhaps, at times, we create our monsters by becoming theirs.

I am rambling. Maybe even losing my mind. It is time for me to make a decision. I cannot help but think of Jesus, Son Of God, who wept during His distress in the Garden Of Gethsemane. He knew the violent death that awaited Him. Now, I face such violence. Last night, I begged God to find some purpose the isle might serve for the betterment of humankind, lest He curse this wretched place and eradicate it from the face of the earth. The latter may indeed come to pass. A great storm is approaching. The darkest clouds are cast overhead, and I hear the waves crashing against the shorelines. The wind is beginning to howl like wolves in mourning. Now, I will rise, open the sanctuary doors, and go forth to meet my fate. I leave this place in the hands of our Lord. Thy will be done, O God.

Professor Amani's Research

I scoured high and low for clues that might help uncover the island's history. I came upon a plethora of writings, documents, and other items that collectively form a story of what occurred here. Two particular sets of records seem to summarize it best.

The first is a series of letters sent between two governing officials involved in bringing humans to the isle. Thankfully, Dr. Radison copied many of his outgoing letters so I could assess the correspondence with greater context. The second critical piece of documentation is a journal kept by Father Abraham, a kindhearted priest who hoped to bring healing to the island.

Background

Raven Island existed off the coast of Massachusetts, United States of America. Dr. Nathaniel Radison, under orders from the state government, used the land as a place to punish, if not rehabilitate, those accused of witchcraft or unholy beliefs. Many perished, having undergone experimental treatments that amounted to torture, brainwashing, humiliation, and mutilation. Those who failed to comply were executed. Sometimes in front of their fellow captives. The prisoners mutinied and gained control of the island. They murdered Dr. Radison and were themselves put to death once reinforcements arrived.

Long after the isle's abandonment, a new attempt was made to revive it by establishing a regular citizenry there. The old institution was set to be restored—the intent being that it might someday be converted into a medical hospital, replacing the meager clinic. Houses were built, and small shops opened for business. They tried to bring modern electricity, though unsuccessfully. A church was established too. Father Abraham arrived on the isle shortly after.

Father Abraham came with the true love of Christ in his heart. He discouraged his congregation from being judgmental and preached against hate and intolerance. Abraham had sympathy for those who suffered at the hands of his religion, and he sought to bring redemption for its wrongdoings. But he alone was not enough to lift the veil of darkness looming over the island. He perished at the hands of a violent cult. As did the remainder of those who stood with him.

Findings

Several things make Raven Island unusual. There's a significant corvid population here, which lends to its name. The weather is dark and gloomy at all times, without ceasing. There are types of seaweed and insects that do not originate in the United States, never mind Massachusetts. Its beaches frequently collect the wreckage of ships that depart from ports around the world. Its inhabitants are gone, and only corpses remain.

There are what appear to be supernatural occurrences as well. Events take place that defy the laws of physics. Strange creatures and apparitions roam the landscape. The animals are often aggressive and act in ways not characteristic of their species. One might even catch glimpses of a massive arachnid that stalks about, hunting prey, mostly in the fog and late at night.

I've gone to the institution, or asylum, on only two occasions. I found it a confusing place that could not decide if it was to be an elegant mansion or a place for the sick. It captured Dr. Radison's personality quite well: the sophisticate and the madman. On my second visit, I felt an evil presence lingering there that unsettled me; it got under my skin to the point I could no longer bear to stay.

While scavenging the isle, I found notes and artifacts pointing toward the Moores, a couple who lived here before Father Abraham arrived. They practiced dark arts and manipulated the townsfolk. When they saw the priest had come, they found it a threat to their plans—so they took action, which led to the massacre Father Abraham spoke of in his journal.

Others like me find themselves stranded here. They come from every part of the world and speak different languages. Each one I meet inevitably encounters the mystic Riel. Like me, they are sent to places on the island where they must confront themselves before they are provided an opportunity to leave. Some are successful. Others are not.

There always seems to be enough food and water available to me. It doesn't make sense, but I consistently find something to eat or drink, no matter how much I've combed through things. Sometimes, even the same container will have something in it after enough time has passed. It's the reason I'm still alive to document it.

Hypothesis

I believe that Raven Island is a spiritual battleground. From its inception, evil has been a part of its foundation. Evils were enacted in the name of that which is good and more evils were taken up as an answer to the injustices inflicted. Father Abraham's attempt to bring light to the dark stirred dormant evil, and there was not enough good on the isle to prevent it from spreading. Thus, it reclaimed this place.

However, in Abraham's last moments, when the island was not unlike the Biblical cities of Sodom and Gomorrah, the weary priest requested that God either use the isle for good or destroy it. As stated in the last page of his journal, a great storm came. I don't know what transpired in that storm. While I don't believe the cultists survived the event, I do think their spirits were trapped here, and their victims moved on.

I also theorize that the island moves about. Before my arrival, I never saw it on any map. This correlates with its ability to transcend what we know of time, space, and the laws of physics. For example, I mentioned in my findings that ships and various forms of seaweed wash up on the shores, far from their native seas. And, of course, some people find themselves stranded here within days of those from different parts of the world. I think the island drifts about the world in no perceivable order, like the ghosts who wander it. Akin to a myth or some mirage you're never sure is there—wiped from history books and maps and minds.

In conclusion, I believe there is a God who eradicated all life on the island. He banished it to continuous exile, forever stuck in constant despair. Not yet doomed to Hell, but in a state of unending purgatory. He uses it as a place to offer redemption, where those on the verge of throwing away their lives receive a sobering last chance to reclaim them. Drawing us to the sea, where this wandering isle ensnares us. Where we can either learn from the didactics given or perish. I don't know where the souls of those who die here go. I think most move on to their respective afterlives. But I once saw a broken soul remain. They joined the spirits who lurk here.

Professor Amani's Note

I have overstayed my time on the island. I should have left while I had the chance. I've been sick the last few days—pneumonia, I think. I can't find any antibiotics in the clinic or remedies in the apothecary. Food has always appeared when needed most, as a courtesy of the Lord, I suppose. But no medicine. Perhaps God is calling me to Him since I neglected to leave when instructed to. I may die in a poorly lit cellar, but a warmer, brighter place awaits me—I believe that.

So now, all there is for me to do is rest and wait. Maybe Riel will come to say goodbye before I go. Should anyone find this, please take whatever supplies I have left. Good luck and Godspeed.

—*Jarad Amani*

Promise

T he night was cold. The survivors pulled near
to each other beneath thick, dusty blankets.
They looked like deer, bedded in low brush,
resting but alert. Frigid air pushed through every
aperture in the house. Faint traces of their breaths
emerged before their faces, and shivers crawled along
their bodies. There was a stove for burning wood.
Though wood lay stacked alongside it, the survivors
knew better than to set it alight. They had seen with
their own eyes what violent fates might be bestowed
upon them for a single misstep. Out there in the
moonlit gloom, devils hunted them. Jackals stalking
amidst vapid plains and rotting boneyards. "I knew
there was something spiritual about this place,"
Makoto said, "but not..." He trailed off, searching for
a word.

"Biblical?" Cody asked. Makoto nodded.

"Havin spent a lot of my life in and out of churches, I figured it might be somethin like that. But it's still a lot to take in."

"It feels like a dream," said Lyssa.

"You mean a nightmare," Rue replied.

"What about you, Koto?" asked Cody. "Havin grew up in Japan, were you raised Shinto? Does any of this fit with your beliefs?"

"My grandparents practiced it," he answered. "My mother too, though she admired your Christ. She helped a friend feed the homeless at a Catholic mission from time to time."

"How about your old man?"

"My father?"

"Yeah, your pa—what'd he believe in?"

"Yakuza was his religion."

"That's the Japanese mafia, right?" asked Rue. Makoto nodded.

"That how you got to working for em?" Cody continued.

"My mother left when I was young. She didn't condone my father's work and begged him to stop. He refused. One day, she got the idea to go to the police for help. She never came home."

"You think she—"

"I don't think it. I know it."

"I'm sorry, son."

Makoto returned a slight smile. It could not conceal his sadness. "My father raised me after that," he said. "He insisted I do well in school so I might have an advantage over other young Yakuza recruits. He was right. But at what cost? I did terrible things that hurt good people, like that man in the recording. All for those who would eventually turn on me. That's how I got here. I ran away. Snuck onto a freight ship and hid until they stopped looking for me. Of course, I had no idea it was about to leave port."

Cody shook his head. "And now you're stuck sleepin on a cold hard floor with an old geezer who asks too many questions," he said.

There was a brief silence, broken by the sound of a cap unscrewing. Lyssa removed the lid from the flask. She extended her arm across the other survivors and handed it to Makoto. He grinned and savored a swig and swallowed it. He passed the flask back to Lyssa. She drank with him.

The survivors slept. Rue woke in the night and found Lyssa staring into the dark. There was a blank expression on her face. "Are you okay?" Rue whispered as she drew closer.

"I don't think so," Lyssa answered.

"What's wrong?"

"I'm scared."

"Of your truth?"

"Yeah."

"It'll be okay, Lys. Try not to worry too much."

"I just have an awful feeling about it. I don't know why. I felt awful about it as soon as Riel told me."

"But why?"

"Because he said I'll find my truth in an asylum, Rue. What if I'm completely batshit crazy? What if Dolion is right and there's something wrong with me, or I'm some bad omen? When Faina died, I realized how much I care about you—about Cody and Koto. The thought of me putting any of you in danger is fucking terrifying."

Rue rested her chin on Lyssa's shoulder. "I don't know what will happen when you find your truth, but we'll be there for you whatever it is. You know we will. And we'll get through it together."

"Promise?"

"Promise."

Lyssa slipped her hand into her pocket and withdrew something. She gave it to Rue. "A bracelet?" Rue asked, studying it.

"I know it's not much. But I want you to have it."

"Lyssa, did you make this?"

"I used some scraps I found in the leather shop."

"I love it."

Lyssa smiled, but the smile faded as she fought back tears. "I don't know why, but I wanted to die before I met you."

"Please, don't say things like that."

"Rue, I mean it. I was drawn to death when I woke up on the island. I'm like a moth to a flame when it comes to things like that. I'm sure there's a reason—something from my past. But the reasons don't really matter, do they? Only that I've changed my mind."

"What do you mean?"

Lyssa let out a weary sigh. "I guess I'm just trying to say thank you," she said.

"For what?"

"For helping me find a reason to live."

Asylum

The passage from night to morning was imperceptible. The gray gloom that canopied the isle was darker now than any day prior, and the rain had worsened. The survivors strode cautiously through the thickening fog. Low-rolling thunder droned on in the distance. It was sonorous and forceful and hung overhead, evincing a brooding wrath that waited to erupt like some landfill dog pulling against a threadbare leash. The gates that sat before the old institution were tall and wide. They were made of faded black iron that choked beneath dead vines. The gates were ajar, and Makoto and Cody pushed them open.

The hinges let out a squeal that transmuted into a grinding moan. The four passed through the gate and stood before the asylum with dread. They leered vexatiously at the castle-like structure before them. Stone gargoyles were perched upon roof ledges. Rows of tall, curtainless windows lined the exterior. They looked like black voids from which Rue thought something stared out at her. In the courtyard was an empty fountain, weathered and discolored. At the center of it set the statue of an angel. The sculptured figure appeared weary and downtrodden and was draped over a black boulder. On the boulder, an engraving read:

Only if thou repent thy sins
shall thy sins be washed away.

Rue wondered how many innocents were led past these words before being forced to confess to sins they never committed. As the survivors walked beyond the fountain to the imposing doors of the Asylum, Cody paused. "Listen," he said, "if anythin happens to me in there, I just want y'all to know I love you like my own kids and grandkids, okay?"

"Thanks, Dad," Makoto replied.

"Yeah, thanks, Grandpa," added Rue.

Lyssa stood silent and turned to the others, an anxious look on her face. "Hey, come here," Rue said as she wrapped her arms around her. Cody threw his arms around the women and embraced them too. Makoto placed his hand over Lyssa's shoulder. He gripped it gently in solidarity.

"Thanks, guys," she said. "Thanks for sticking with me."

Makoto grabbed the handles of the large, ornate door of the institute. "Everyone ready?" he asked. They each nodded, and Makoto pushed open the door. It made a dense clacking sound followed by a resounding creak.

There was darkness on the other side of the door, yet the faint, natural light lifted shadows from the entryway. Makoto switched on the flashlight. The survivors watched scrupulously as the beam swept over an enormous staircase. There were long halls that extended in all directions. Paintings hung along the walls. A rhythmic burst of luminous white light flooded the building, and a deafening crack of thunder erupted. The rain poured harder, drumming loudly upon the asylum.

A banquet hall was at the end of the main corridor. Inside it, many tables and chairs lay broken and in piles. In the middle of the room was a grand piano. Lyssa ran one finger over the keys, but they no longer formed a melodic sound. Instead, her taps made muted thuds that spat dust from the crevices between the keys. "It's a shame it's broken," Lyssa said. "It would have been lovely to hear."

The group continued exploring the institution. They found the first floor composed of rooms and accommodations for the staff who had lived there. Still, there was no sign of Lyssa's truth. They agreed to search the next level and started up the stairs toward the second floor. At the top of the staircase, an eerie painting towered over them. It depicted a white raven sitting atop a human skull in an ocean of blood, and though the artwork was old, its scarlet paint appeared wet and runny, as though it might drip over the lower portion of the frame. A plaque on the bottom read:

Salvation | Nathaniel Radison

The survivors began searching the second floor. The walls were encrusted with filth and grime. The wallpaper peeled like bark from a birch tree, and vestiges of footprints were smeared into the greasy floors. Several rooms were no more than open spaces filled with poorly assembled beds. They were covered in defiled, dirty bedding reduced to little more than rags. A doll crafted from scraps of feculent bed coverings and human hair lay atop a thin mattress. Its eyes and features were made of pebbles and dry beans.

In the hall, Lyssa stepped through a doorway into another room. Rue followed, but the door slammed in her face. Lyssa screamed from the other side. "Lyssa, open the door!" Rue shouted. She watched the door handle turn and jerk about, but the door was stuck.

"I'm fucking trying!" Lyssa replied, panic sinking in. Makoto slammed his shoulder against the door. He kicked repeatedly below the handle. It would not budge.

"Are you still there?" Rue called out. There was no answer.

"Wait, what's that sound?" asked Makoto.

"What sound?" replied Cody.

"Listen—I think it's coming from downstairs."

"It's the piano," Rue answered.

"But the thing didn't even work," Cody said.

They looked at each other in disbelief as Beethoven's "Moonlight Sonata" played on the untuned piano, the music reverberating from the lower floor. There was another flash of lightning. Rue could see shadowed figures staring at her from down the hallway. Their eyes glowing white like those she had seen on the beach. Then they were gone. "Did you see that?" she asked as she pointed down the hall.

"See what?" Cody asked.

"There were people—ghosts, whatever!"

"Where'd they go?"

"I don't know," Rue said. "They were there one second and gone the next."

"We need to get Lyssa out of this room," Makoto urged.

"But how?"

"We need to find something we can use to break down the door or find anothe—"

Before Makoto could finish, an unseen force hurled him across the hallway. He tumbled down the stairs. Rue shrieked and chased after him, but a spectral wave of pressure drove her up against the wall. Cody reached for her but was yanked to the floor and dragged away. Rue tried to fight against the hold on her. It was no use. She was pulled along the wall opposite her friends. She felt pressure form around her neck that was familiar to her. She knew not why. Everything went black.

Rue opened her eyes. She was in a part of the asylum where she had not yet been. Alone and without her flashlight, she withdrew the lighter from her pocket. She prayed fluid was still inside as she sparked a flame with her thumb and held it before her. In the dim light could be seen a room once destroyed by fire. Ash lay like snow along the blackened floor. Rue crept into an adjoining room and stood near a tall window. She peered outside as rain ran down the weathered glass. She was on the third floor. *Shit*, Rue thought, *how did I get all the way up here?*

Rue stepped into the hallway to search for a way downstairs. She heard footsteps scampering ahead of her in the dark. With each movement she made, they grew closer. Feminine laughter subtly echoed. Rue continued sneaking further down the hall, wincing at every creak of the floorboards beneath her feet. A deep rumble of thunder bellowed outside. Lightning flashed again. When the flutter of light was cast against the asylum, a face peeked out from behind a corner. A moment later, it moved back out of sight. Rue stood there timorous and shaking and thought she might drop the lighter.

Each passing moment felt like ages come and gone. The relentless sound of raindrops drubbing upon the roof was all she could hear. A terrifying caterwaul broke the quiet calm as feet pounded along the floor. It was coming right for her. She tried to run, but a woman leaped from the dark and slashed at her with a knife. Rue yelped. She drew back and gripped her forearm and saw blood seeping through a tear in her sleeve. Rue looked up to see the woman's face and was horrified.

Lyssa stood there in the dark hallway. She spoke incoherently in broken sentences. She waved the knife as though another stood before her, but no one was there. Her jacket was gone. Her feet were bare. She wore only her torn black dress. "Lyssa," Rue said, "it's me!" Lyssa stopped talking. She stood motionless, staring at nothing. Her mouth still moved, forming words that no longer made sound. "Lyssa?" Rue tried again.

In a soft, cyclic manner, Lyssa giggled and cried and returned to murmuring. Rue reached out to touch

Lyssa's arm, but she lashed out at her. "I'll kill you!" she screamed. "I'll fucking kill everyone!" Lyssa slashed at Rue's face, and she dodged the arc of the swing. She scrambled past Lyssa and ran down the hall. Rue grabbed hold of a door handle as Lyssa chased behind her. There was a crack of thunder, and she saw Lyssa closing in on her in the momentary glow of white light. She screamed and laughed in psychotic paroxysms as a glint of light caught the blade of her bloody knife. Rue shut the door and leaned all her weight into it. Lyssa rapped violently on it from the other side. She thrashed and hollered as Rue planted her feet to brace herself, her shoes sliding on the grimy floor.

"Lyssa, stop," she pleaded. "Please stop and talk to me!"

There was a sudden pause in Lyssa's attack. Rue could hear her whispering to someone on the other side. It was a voice she did not recognize. She thought she might crack open the door to see but found the door locked from the outside. "Hey!" she shouted. She tried forcing the door handle, but it would not turn.

There was enough light from the window that Rue could see the faint arrangement of the room. She surmised it was a study. There was a large table covered in old parchment and ink bottles where a quill was once dabbed. Bookcases lined one wall. Strange artwork hung upon the other. Rue searched for a key, and when no key was found, she scavenged for a tool with which she might pry open the door. She fumbled through a desk drawer. It was filled with stationary. There was a slow creak behind her, and she turned to see that one of the bookcases had moved. Behind it, a hidden passage stood agape. *Hell no, do I really have to go in there?* Rue thought. *I guess I should know better than to ask.*

Rue nervously stepped into the corridor behind the bookcase. There were cobwebs stretched throughout. One wall was built from wood planks, and between the planks were gaps. She could see nothing through the cracks but darkness. She moved slowly along the opposite wall, keeping her back to it as she held the lighter ahead of her. The corridor narrowed with each step until her chest grazed the plank wall. In the pitch black behind the wooden boards, she could see the vague shapes of human faces. They grinned with malice.

Rue heard a sharp breath like that of someone extinguishing a candle, and the flame of her lighter was gone. She let out a frantic gasp. Hands groped at her, from her face to her feet. She tried not to scream, but she could not contain her terror. Rue squeezed herself through the corridor as fast as she could. She struggled to control her breathing as she fought the wave of panic that overcame her. A moment later, she was free from her confinement.

Rue found herself inside a space no larger than a closet. There was nothing but a ladder that extended down through a shaft in the floor. *I've got to stop assuming it can't get any worse,* she thought. She mustered her courage once more and descended the ladder. The wooden rungs were worn and cracked, and each one bowed beneath her weight. The ladder seemed to go on forever. She looked down into the dark below, and a deep cackle echoed throughout the shaft. It was all she could do to keep going. When she heard it a second time, she stopped climbing. She considered going back. There was no going back. The rung beneath her foot gave way, snapping in half. Rue's body jerked downward, and she dangled there by one hand. She tried to swing her other hand up to grab the rung above her, but it gave way too. She fell down the shaft violently.

Rue moaned in pain from the harsh impact. "What's the matter, girl?" asked a sinister voice. "Never used a ladder before?"

Another chimed in. "I hope the bitch broke her back."

And then another. "Let's pull off her arms and legs as the dogs did to her friend."

They laughed, and Rue could sense them surrounding her. She could see their silhouettes and their evil eyes, glowing in the dark as they had before. Panic came over her again. Her breaths were fast and shallow. The voices continued.

"Let's feed her to the spider."

"Watch it suck her guts out."

"Why let that thing have all the fun? We can play with her for days."

"How much blood do you think she has in her?"

"Shut up!" Rue screeched. She flicked the wheel of the lighter. "Get away from me!"

She flailed the lighter about with wild abandon, hoping she might create distance from the apparitions. Wherever the light was not, the eyes lingered. She could see them observing her from the corners of the room. Rue moved throughout the space, and something dawned on her; this was the dungeon in which the warden experimented on prisoners. There were gore-filled jail cells and splintering stockades. Operating tables with leather straps. Rusted tools and torture apparatuses were carelessly strewn about. Blood was smeared across every surface.

Rue ran through room after room. Corridor after corridor. The longer she ran, the louder and more wicked the voices grew. She leaped over desiccated corpses and trudged through severed limbs. Startled bats flitted across her face. When she reached the far end of the dungeon, a slim beam of light poked through a wooden board nailed across a narrow opening where the wall met the ceiling. Rue dragged an empty crate below it. She clawed at the plank's edges, praying she might get her fingers behind it to pry it from the wall. Demonic hands grabbed and scratched at her legs. She screamed in terror. A familiar voice shouted to her from the other side of the plank as something slammed against it from the outside. Then again and again. On the fourth strike, Rue ducked her head. Makoto's foot kicked through the opening, knocking the plank to the floor. He and Cody each extended their hands and pulled Rue up through the opening and out of the basement dungeon. She gasped and collapsed onto her hands and knees. As she caught her breath in the pouring rain, Rue grabbed hold of her friends. She wept.

Denial

Rue anxiously stared up at the asylum. Her eyes scanned each window in hurried sweeps, moving from floor to floor. In none did she see Lyssa's face peering back at her. "She isn't in there," Makoto said.

"We saw her runnin out the front," added Cody. "We called for her to come back, but she didn't seem to hear us—probably on account of the thunder and rain."

"We've got to find her," Rue said urgently. "Something happened to her in there, and she needs us."

"We will," Makoto replied, "but we should keep going for now. We don't know if Lyssa found her truth yet, but if she did, it means that yours is the last one. From what Riel told you, it isn't much farther, right?"

"Yeah, he said it's just beyond the Asylum. But we can't just leave her."

"You have my word," Cody said, "we ain't leavin the island without findin her and figurin out what happened. We made it this far together. We ain't leavin each other behind."

Rue nodded. "I just don't understand what came over her," she said.

"There's a lot of evil in this place," replied Makoto. "Who knows what got to her while she was alone in that room."

"I guess you're right," Rue said defeatedly.

"Come on. We're going to finish this, okay?"

"Okay."

The survivors trudged through the muddy soil and watched for dangers around them. They knew not where they were headed except that a house lay beyond the institute, and in this house was Rue's truth for which they had come all this way. The sky continued growing darker, as though the short days of the island were relinquishing to eternal nightfall. Rue shivered. Her clothes were drenched. Cody and Makoto were miserable too. They walked in their soused shoes and soaked jackets but did their best to conceal their discomfort.

Men, Rue thought. *They forget it's okay to show a little weakness from time to time.* Still, she respected their effort. She found her friends' commitment to feigning strength assuaging in her moments of vulnerability, for she longed to be fearless and wondered now if courage was simply a mask or perhaps some parlor trick meant to distract from what lies beneath it. Surrendering in fear to all outcomes and fighting desperately for the one the heart most desires. Rue was terrified of the isle. She always had been. Yet her will to live masqueraded as a beguiling veil of confidence that tunneled her vision toward her instinctual goal of self-preservation. As she considered this, she thought of how wounded animals hide their pain and fear to deter predators and how they might lash out or flee if confronted. Fight or flight was not courage or cowardice. It was an impulsive reaction embedded into her subconscious after a lifetime of conditioning.

Her past, though unremembered, haunted her very being.

The rain softened as they walked. A shape began to emerge on the horizon, and the survivors drew closer. They could see a house set in a grassy meadow. Each step they took swelled the house into view, along with the stifling weight of disquietness. "You okay?" Cody asked. Rue shook her head. "Try not to worry, darlin."

"That's what I told Lyssa," Rue replied.

"Fair point."

"Do you think it was Lyssa's truth?"

"What do you mean?"

"That made her act like that."

"I reckon it's possible."

"Oh."

Cody shook his head. "These truths ain't easy for any of us. They show us things about ourselves—about our pasts. Ugly things we wouldn't look at. Tried to run from. Whatever her truth was, it might have been more than she was ready for. More than she could face alone anyhow."

"Do you think that will happen to me too?"

"This time, we'll make sure we stay together. Me and Koto will do everything we can to keep you grounded."

Rue nodded. "I heard her talking to someone after she chased me into a room," she said. "I couldn't hear anyone speaking to her, but she was speaking to them."

"Like Koto said earlier, that asylum is an evil place. Lord only knows what got in her ear while she was alone in there."

"I hope we can find her again."

"We will, darlin. You best believe we will."

They entered the front yard and looked at the middling home. They felt a relentless sorrow emanating from it. Rue stood staring at the doorway. Makoto offered a slight yet reassuring smile. He handed her the flashlight, and she pushed open the door and went inside.

A familiar aroma filled her nostrils. She did not know it, but it smelled like home. There were no furnishings in the house, spare a tattered blue couch. On it lay a teddy bear. One arm was torn at the shoulder, and stuffing stuck out from the tear. Its tan fur was stained with blood. A wave of regret overtook Rue as she approached it. She lifted the stuffed animal into her arms, and instantly, memories cascaded into her mind, a slipstream surging beneath a fathomless deluge. One memory rose from her subconscious above all others. She tried to resist, though she did not know why. But her efforts were in vain. It was her truth, the reason she was there.

Rue's Memory

Rue was late getting home. It was a clear, warm evening, and she had worked a busy shift waiting tables at the Market Street Diner. She took with her a fair sum of generous tips. More than she had made in months. When she arrived at the street on which she lived, she was startled by red and blue lights oscillating along the blacktop. They splashed against every surface in the neighborhood. In front of her home, police swarmed the lawn. They traipsed in and out of the house like ants passing to and fro. She parked her car and opened the driver door and an officer gestured in her direction. Without hesitation, a detective trotted toward her. He threw his hand up and waved off the officers seeking his attention. "Ma'am, do you live here?" he asked.

"Yes," she said, "that's my house."

Sirens blared in the distance. They grew louder with each passing second. "I'm Detective Mitch White." Rue paused, tension building inside her. "You have a little girl?" he continued.

"Y-yes," Rue answered. Her heart was racing. She saw her boyfriend being escorted from the house in handcuffs. As they made eye contact, he shot her a callus grin. "W-where's my daughter?" Rue asked anxiously.

"Ma'am," said the detective as the ambulance pulled in front of the property, "I'm gonna need you to come down to the station with me. Can you do that?"

"I need to see my daughter."

"I'm afraid that's not possible right now."

"No, don't say that shit to me!"

"Ma'am, trust me, it's better this way. I'll answer all your questions when we get to the station."

Rue nodded reluctantly.

At the police station, Rue was sat in a room used to interview witnesses. An officer offered something to drink, but she refused. She sat for what felt like an eternity. Thirty minutes had passed before Detective White came in to see her. He walked in and stood across from her at the table. He sat for a moment, glancing between Rue and a file he laid on the tabletop. Her head was hung. Her arms were folded tight as if to shield herself from what he would say. White pitied her. He stood back up and carried his chair to the other side of the table and set it down next to Rue. He sat back down again, this time leaning toward her. "Is it okay if I call you Rue?" he asked. Rue nodded. "Rue, I've got something I need to tell you. It won't be easy to hear."

"Is she okay?"

"No."

"Please don't say it."

White paused and weighed his words. "This thing you don't want me to say..."

"Yeah?"

"I think you know what it is and why we're here, but I still need to say it anyway. I need to make sure you understand, okay?"

Rue nodded again, wincing in anticipation.

"Your daughter passed away today."

Rue moaned distressingly, and White continued. "She passed before the police arrived."

Rue burst into tears. Detective White handed her a box of tissues. "I'm so sorry," he said. "I know it hurts."

Rue continued to sob. "How long have you been with your boyfriend?" White asked.

Rue looked up at him. He could see the frustration and guilt and anger surfacing behind her dark, teary eyes. "Long enough to know it was him," she answered.

"What makes you say that?"

"He's a monster."

"Yes. Yes, he is."

"How bad was it?"

White paused again. He took a deep breath. "It was bad."

"How bad?"

"Really fucking bad."

Rue cried harder and slammed her fist down on the table. She wiped her eyes and nose with the tissues as she struggled to keep herself together. A few minutes passed. "What did he tell you?" she asked.

"Your daughter was deaf, is that right?"

"Yeah, but she could sign."

"And your boyfriend—he doesn't know how to sign?"

"He didn't want to learn."

"Why not?"

Rue choked back her tears. "He said it was a dumb way to speak for people too stupid to hear."

White bitterly shook his head, almost in disbelief. "From what we gather," he continued, "he came home a few hours before we arrived. He was drunk. We believe he had cocaine in his system as well."

"Sounds like him."

"You do any drugs, Rue?"

"No."

White nodded. "We're not sure what transpired exactly, but it appears something triggered him into a sort of rage, at which point he became extremely violent. Apparently, while like this, he told your daughter to do something. We think she had her back to him, and since she couldn't hear, she didn't acknowledge him. That's when he got upset and attacked her."

"Please, stop," Rue said. White nodded. "Just tell me," she asked, "did she suffer?"

White paused, looking away. He took a deep breath and exhaled and looked back at her sorrowfully. "I'm afraid so," he replied.

Rue felt her despair take hold. Before she could give in to it, White distracted her with another question. "Rue, if you don't mind me asking, may I see your arms?"

"What?"

"Can you pull up your sleeves?"

"I, um—"

"Rue, he can't hurt you anymore."

Rue hesitated, then drew back her sleeves. Her forearms were flecked with deep bruises. Some big, some small. They were shades of yellow and black and blue. "I'm gonna guess you've got more of those all over?" White asked.

Her voice cracked. "Yeah," she answered.

Rue cried for almost an hour. Makoto and Cody stayed close to her as she told them her story. She told them how her boyfriend abused her and murdered her daughter. She spoke of how her family and friends pleaded with her to leave him, but against her better judgment, she stayed. How her estranged father taught her survival in the wilderness but not how a man should respect a woman in the home. Rue said Lyssa was right; she was too naive and mailable. She could finally see the hurt her denial caused to those she loved most. "I was too afraid to leave or stand up for myself," she said. "Too afraid to make my own decisions. And my daughter paid the price for it."

"Maybe so," replied Cody, "But bein on this island must've been changin you—even before you found out about your past."

"What do you mean?"

"I mean, since we met, you been anything but that."

"He's right," Makoto added. "You didn't hold back from giving Dolion a piece of your mind. And you took the lead when Riel told you about the house with the cellar."

"Yeah, maybe," Rue replied. "I guess this place has been working on all of us."

"I think so," Cody said.

Rue held the stuffed bear in her hands. She looked at the dried blood matted in the fabric. "I just wish I could go back in time."

Cody nodded. "Me too, darlin. Me too."

"What would you do if you could?"

"I would never use my reptilian ex-wife as an excuse to bottle up my feelins. I bottled em up until I had nowhere to go except to crawl inside a bottle myself. Yeah, I reckon I'd do a lot of things differently."

"What about you, Koto?" Rue asked.

Makoto thought for a moment. "I wouldn't take any money from that shop owner," he said. "I would ask him for a job instead."

Rue smiled. "I like that."

"Can I ask you a question now?"

"Okay."

"How'd you wind up here?"

Rue paused to remember. A moment later, the memory was there again, like it had never been gone at all. "I didn't know what to do with myself after my daughter died. One afternoon, I walked out my front door and just wandered for hours. Eventually, I came across a quiet inlet. There was this empty little boat there. Barely room enough for two people. I didn't see anyone around who it might've belonged to, so I just laid in it and looked up at the sky. At some point, I dozed off. You can probably guess what happened after that."

Hurt

Thunder cracked and rolled like a gliding wave passing over the isle. Lightning frayed between the earth and the sky. Radiant fractures in a glass pane. The downpour was back. The survivors readied to return to the village and stepped out of the house. Riel spoke to Rue once more. *If you're to understand your friend,* he said, *go back to the asylum.* She told this to the others who were reluctant to enter the asylum again. Yet they agreed. They trudged through the deepening mire toward the place from which they came.

Night had fallen by the time the structure entered their view. Darkness was of little difference to them now, for they were determined not to spend one day more on the island. *Once we find Lyssa, we can help her,* Rue thought, *and Riel can finally show us the way home.*

They approached from behind the institution and crept along its perimeter, observing what dangers awaited them. It was unsettlingly quiet. Makoto shined the flashlight inside the entryway, sweeping the beam across the room as he had before. "I really hate this place," he said.

"You're telling me?" Rue replied.

"I dunno about y'all," added Cody, "but I think Beethoven might be ruined for me after this." Everyone nodded.

"So where to now?" Makoto asked.

"Riel didn't say," answered Rue, "but if I had to guess, we should try the room she was locked in before we all got ghosted."

They ascended the stairs and noticed that the painting they saw earlier had changed. There was nothing but black paint where the image once was. The floor beneath was stained with blood, and in the center of the stain lay a skull. It was as though the image itself washed into their reality, and Rue pondered the ways in which the place had come to life while they were there. The asylum was now as quiet as the spirits who lurked in it. She dreaded their presence, yet the absence equally terrified her. Somewhere on the path between death and life, they waited like vipers in a rosebush. Only the most unwavering travelers might pass unscathed, lest they perish by their own credulity.

When they reached the door to the room where Lyssa had been locked inside, they found it open. Her leather jacket and black boots were piled on the floor. A thin book was set atop the windowsill with a folded paper tucked inside the rear cover.

Lyssa's Diary

Entry 1.

Yesturday Santa Claws came to the orfanidge and gave all the kids dyaries. It was so cool! Emily says there is no Santa but she is wrong. She is just mad becaws mine is prety and hers is sooo ugly. Maybe Santa hates her caws she piks her nose and puts it on our sheets and tells Miss Holly it was us. Katie asked Emily why she dos it and she said so she can pik on us and then she laffed in Katies face. Emily is gross and I hope she gets adopted by trolls and gets eated.

Entry 2.

Tomorrow I am going to a new foster home. These foster parents seem ok but I don't know. They are kind of weird and I don't like how they look at me. They say they have a few other kids my age: two girls who are 8 and 10 and two boys who are 9 and 11. I hope we can all be friends. The last foster home was a bad place.

Entry 3.

Today is my birthday. I'm 14 now. Hannah gave me my first cigarette, and I nearly coughed my damn lungs up. It sucked, but at the same time, I liked the taste and the smell. I don't know why. Anyway, she said she'll get me more after she talks to some kid she knows at school. I guess I should also mention that Tyler ran away. Can I blame him? The house is filthy and cold, and the Bradwells treat us like shit. Mr. Bradwell always tries to touch us and force us to do nasty things. He makes gross comments whenever he sees us. Mrs. Bradwell isn't any better. She's a hateful, psychotic bitch. Every year, I swear, she gets worse. I try to avoid them and drown them out with my music. It usually works. Until it doesn't.

Entry 4.

I hate this stupid fucking place! Last night, the Bradwells managed to get everyone out of the house except for me, and those psychos put something in my food. The next thing I knew, I was tied to my bed. They found my cigarettes and said they needed to punish me for acting out, so they smoked my cigs in front of me and snuffed them out on my body. I screamed and begged them to stop. They just laughed. Then they took turns sticking their fat fucking fingers in me. It only got worse after that—fucking animals! If I ever find where either of those dumb cows keeps their gun, I'll blow a hole through their heads wider than their "disability" checks. Or maybe I'll just kill myself instead. What's the point of being alive if this is all there is?

Entry 5.

There's a new kid in the house. His name is Garrett. He's sixteen, which is one year older than me. We have a lot in common. He listens to the same music and likes all the same books and movies. We tend to share the same ideas about things too. How's the saying go? Oh yeah, we get along like a house on fire— that's the one. I also appreciate that Garrett doesn't take any shit from the Bradwells. He distracted them on more than one occasion so the rest of us could slip out for a while. I've had poor experiences with most men I've met, yet Garrett's not like them. He's sensitive and kind but isn't afraid to fight for what he wants. I like that. He's also quite handsome. I like that too.

Entry 6.

It's been two months since Garrett arrived, and I think I'm falling for him. We've been almost inseparable since we met. He hasn't been a creep to me. Nothing other than a perfect gentleman. Yet he has his dark side—his edge. We drown out our worries together with whatever cheap booze we can get our hands on. We share smokes and lie on our backs, gazing at the moon. We talk about poetry and discuss our dreams. Sometimes, we wonder if there's an afterlife and if it's actually any better than this one. I've found that the more intolerable life becomes, the more comforting the idea of non-existence is to me. Though, for the first time, I feel like living might not be so bad after all.

Entry 7.

Shit hit the fan today. Mr. Bradwell made one of his usual advances on me, and I scratched his face. I didn't see it coming when he drove his fist into my stomach. I yelped, then gasped. It knocked the wind right out of me. The sound I made must have been louder than I thought because Garrett rushed down the stairs and burst into the room. Mr. Bradwell warned him to stay back, and they argued while I struggled to catch my breath. Next thing I knew, Garret was beating the living hell out of Mr. Bradwell, and Mrs. Bradwell was screaming about calling the police. Garrett helped me pack my things, and we left. We'd rather be on the street than stay in that house any longer.

Entry 8.

Sorry, diary. I've been busy. Almost a year on the street already. We're mostly sleeping rough, though we do get into shelters once in a while. I'm not sure which is worse. Garrett and I stay close to one another because it's dangerous out here. A lot of men see a sixteen-year-old girl in a bad spot and think they can get her to come home with them by promising a hot meal and a place to shower. Others are less subtle and go straight to touching if they catch me alone, but I'm quick with a knife now. A girl's got to protect herself. By the way, I ran into Tyler, my old foster brother. He said he knows a guy who can get Garret and me into a small flat above the liquor store on 5th and Main. It turns out the landlord owes him a favor. I guess miracles do happen.

Entry 9.

It's been wonderful to finally have a roof over our heads. Garret managed to land a job working security at a retirement home. I'm working at a used bookshop. Hopefully, in time, we'll move on to better things. In the meantime, we're just enjoying our new life together. I'll be eighteen in a few months, but I won't write what that means because I don't want to jinx it.

Entry 10.

We eloped! I can't even believe it—this feels so surreal! Two years ago, I never would've thought this day would come. But here I am, and I can't stop smiling. This is hands down the best day of my life. I only wish I had a family I could celebrate with. I guess that was never really in the cards for me. I'm just glad we have each other.

Entry 11.

Lately, I've been thinking a lot about my parents and how I came to be put into foster care. Garret helped me track down someone at the orphanage. We (drumroll) finally learned where I came from. Sadly, I was better off not knowing.

My mom's name was Natalie. She died during childbirth. Meaning my dad was the one who gave me up for adoption. We couldn't track him down, but we found where he lived while he was with my mom. A few days later, we went to the house. The neighbor happened to be putting her trash cans on the curb. She was an older woman—said she knew my parents and grandparents. She invited us into her home to chat for a while. Told me how my grandfather was a minister and my mom was a meek kid. At seventeen, she began seeing my dad. My grandfather adored him because he went to their church. Supposedly, my dad pressured her into having sex, and she got knocked up. Then things got uglier.

My mom wanted an abortion. She spoke to three doctors. Each confirmed she had medical complications that placed her in the upper percentile for high mortality risk. She was terrified of dying. Still, my grandparents forbade her from going through with the procedure. My father wouldn't allow it either. She sought to do it anyway, but the state legal system prohibited it without spousal or parental support.

My mom died at 8:42 on an otherwise typical Thursday night. It's strange, actually. There was a football game that aired that evening. You'd be surprised how many people remember it. Few remember my mom, though. The best part of this heartwarming tale? My grandparents couldn't bear to look at the child who killed their daughter, and my dad didn't want the responsibility. They thought the system was what I deserved. Now I'll know I'm the reason my mom is dead whenever I look at myself in the mirror. The monster nobody wanted.

Entry 12.

Recently, Garret was fired from his job. They wouldn't tell him why they let him go at first. Then, finally, they admitted it was because some asshole complained about his appearance—said his tattoos and piercings made them feel uncomfortable and that it's an unacceptable look for a security guard. He's always been so kind to the elderly who live there. Management wouldn't even let him finish the rest of the work week. We're already desperate to make ends meet, so I have no idea how we'll pay our bills this month. That said, Garrett knows a guy who might be able to get him a temporary gig on the side. Some fast cash to get us by for a few weeks and hopefully enough time for him to find a new job.

Entry 13.

Fuck—this can't be happening. This can't be happening! Those assholes set him up! They offered Garrett cash to drive a moving truck across town. It was a simple job. He had no idea drugs were stashed inside the boxes they loaded onto it or that the cops had been tipped off and were tracking the vehicle. But the people who hired him knew. They fucking knew it! Now, he's in jail for drug trafficking, and we can't prove his innocence. What are we going to do? How the hell are we supposed to fix this?

Entry 14.

I visited Garrett today at the county jail. He doesn't look good. I've never seen him so stressed or afraid. It looked like he was in a nasty fight. When I asked him what happened, he said people inside have it out for him. I asked why, but he wasn't sure—said some guy made a passing comment about how he better keep his mouth shut. Maybe because he tried telling the cops he was set up? I'm so scared for him. We don't have any money to hire a lawyer or a private investigator. No one will help us. I don't know what to do.

Entry 15.

My life is over. When they told me Garrett was killed, I refused to believe it. But I was the only one who could identify his body, and I had no choice. I was forced to accept that it was him. He was my everything. Now he's gone. Not even his ghost is here to comfort me. All I have left are his ashes, which they uncaringly wrapped up, placed in a coffee-stained cardboard box, and handed to me with the rest of his things. He never got justice. They never even gave him a chance. I want to die. I want to be with him. Wherever that is.

Patient Notes

Michelle Garland (Psy.D)

I met Lyssa for the first time several months ago. She was frail and pitiful in such a way that it surprised me. Never had a patient touched my heart as she did. I knew little about her past, only the crimes for which she was committed to our psychiatric facility. However, as with all my patients, I was determined to get to know her as best I could.

Lyssa was quiet for the first few months. It took time, but she warmed up to me with each session. It was actually Snow, the white raven I keep in my office for company, who helped me get her comfortable enough to talk. We mostly spoke of Snow and other species of corvid at first. She seemed fascinated by them. Then, we discussed literature and the arts. Throughout these conversations, I saw what a humble and bright young woman she was. She never struck me as the type that would do the things she'd done. Yet here she was, a patient said to have lost her mind.

After a while, Lyssa told me about her life as an orphan and the trauma and abuse she suffered from her late foster parents. She told me of her loathing toward herself after learning that her birth caused her mother's death. That her father and grandparents wanted nothing to do with her. We talked about homelessness and how it brought out violent tendencies she later struggled to suppress. Then, the tragic fate of her young husband, Garrett. But I still needed to know what led her to the attempted murder of a whole family.

Lyssa could no longer afford to pay rent when Garrett passed. She was evicted from their apartment. Having nowhere to go, she wandered the streets for several days. She had nothing. Only what she could carry in her backpack. This included the standard-issue plastic bag which contained her husband's cremated remains.

Lyssa stumbled into a church on a bitter autumn evening, hoping to escape the plunging temperatures. She said she sat alone on a pew and debated taking her own life when a member named Teressa approached her. She saw Lyssa was desperate and offered for her to stay with her family while she got back on her feet. Lyssa took this as divine intervention and accepted Teressa's offer.

Things went well for a few weeks. Lyssa started a new job and saved her money while trying her best not to burden Teressa's family. She got along with Teressa's husband, Robert, and her two kids, Timothy and Jennifer. Unfortunately, things quickly fell apart.

Jennifer, who was the same age, began showing a romantic interest in Lyssa. Though still grieving the death of her husband, Lyssa was lonely. She had no close friends. No family. She longed for the comforts of human affection and, in an error of judgment, accepted this affection from Jen. They became intimate.

Meanwhile, Robert had also taken an interest in Lyssa. Late one night, he attempted to engage Lyssa sexually. She rejected the advance. This embarrassed and angered him, and he became paranoid that Lyssa might tell his wife. To gain the upper hand, he lied to

Teressa. He said Lyssa made a pass at him. She fell for it.

To make matters worse, so did Jen. Spiteful and upset, she told her parents Lyssa came onto her too. Lyssa argued in defense of herself, but it made little difference. Teressa didn't believe anything she had to say. She knew nothing of her daughter's sexuality, and despite Lyssa's pleas for Jen to come clean, Jen refused to admit it to her devout parents.

Though they were lies, Teressa was enraged by what her family told her. She saw Lyssa as a threat. Without any warning, she forced her to leave the house. Lyssa stood outside in the cold and begged for her backpack. Several minutes passed, and the front door opened again. Teresa tossed the bag from the porch without ensuring it was zipped shut, and it tumbled through the air. When the backpack hit the ground, its contents were ejected from it. The plastic pouch that held Garrett's remains split from the force of the impact. His ashes scattered across the lawn and were lost in a gust of wind.

Lyssa says she doesn't remember the breakdown she experienced after. So it was at this moment she lost control of herself. The culmination of all her traumas surfaced to the point of a violent blackout. According to the family, she lunged at Teressa, who slammed the door in her face. Lyssa clawed at it with her bare hands until the police came. She fled, only to return late that night. As the family slept, she set fire to their house. She almost killed them.

My heart broke for Lyssa after hearing her story in greater detail. I wanted to focus on helping her heal from her past and did my best to ensure her time here was as pleasant as possible. That way, we could move on to more constructive activities. She made significant progress at first, giving me hope that she was on an effective path toward recovery. I found she smiled more frequently and spoke less nihilistically about her life. But then something changed. I didn't know why, but Lyssa became withdrawn again. She acted more aggressively toward the staff. She barely ate her meals. It wasn't until her escape that I realized—sadly, all too late—what was happening.

Our psychiatric facility lost several nurses all at one time. In desperate need of help, management hastily brought in replacements. Background checks were not handled appropriately, and because of this, they hired a man with a criminal history of sex offenses. He became one of Lyssa's regular nurses. Like so many others, he took advantage of her at every opportunity. That's why she regressed.

Lyssa was always resourceful. On the night of her escape, detectives believe she drank as much as she could and refrained from urinating until it was time for her to retire to her room. She knew the man assaulting her would return after the lights were out and urinated on the floor—right in front of the door. The nurse came into the room and slipped on the wet tile. He hit his head on the door frame and collapsed. I was told that Lyssa grabbed the bottom of his shirt, blinded him with it by pulling it over his head, and kicked his face and groin more than thirty times. He barely survived due to the loss of blood from his head injuries.

Lyssa fled her room and snuck through the hospital until she found an opportunity to escape. No one knows where she went. There were reports of a girl seen nearby matching her description. A clothing store reported that a young woman broke in and stole several items the night Lyssa ran away. A few days later, a truck driver called the police after seeing a woman jump from a bridge into the bay beneath—a distance that would likely be fatal. I can only hope it was an unrelated case and that we might someday meet again. Or she at least finds help wherever she is.

Rue tucked the paper into the journal and placed it back on the windowsill. "No wonder she was acting crazy," Rue said. "All that trauma and grief came back to her all at once, and no one was with her to help her process it. Only the demons who trapped her in here."

"Poor thing was straddlin the edge of insanity the whole time. If only we'd known, we could've tried harder," Cody replied.

"I think she knew something was wrong but wasn't sure what it was. She had a bad feeling about herself. We all wanted to learn our truths, but she dreaded hers. There must have been so much pain buried inside her that, even without her memories, she could still feel its weight crushing her."

"Our truths showed us how our choices hurt those around us," said Makoto. "Lyssa was different. Her suffering caused her to hurt others—even herself."

"I think that's it," Rue replied.

"What do you mean?" asked Cody.

"That's why we were all brought here together at the same time. Lyssa is showing us how to put others above ourselves, and we're showing Lyssa it's not too late for her to find people who care about her. Like she said to me last night—a reason to keep living."

"I reckon you might be right."

"There's only one thing left to do now," said Makoto.

"Let's find her," Rue replied.

Rage

Rue walked determinedly as Makoto and Cody trailed behind her. She gripped the flashlight in her wet hands. Her eyes darted to and from every crooked tree and mossy stone. Every crumbling wall and weather-worn sign. In a flicker of lightning, she thought she saw some foul creature slink into the heart of the village. A full moon hung overhead. It peeked through the dark clouds like a watchful eye peering through a slender keyhole. On the outskirts of the village, the survivors reached the house where they found the secret cellar. They checked inside, hoping that Lyssa had returned. But she was not there.

Outside, six headstones were sunk into the muddy earth. They were not there when they arrived, and they had no markings. Two leaned forward over empty graves, and three more over plots filled with fresh soil. The last headstone had no grave at all. Rue was unsure what to make of it. She felt they were being mocked, and perhaps the three covered graves represented herself and Cody and Makoto.

The survivors pressed on and drew closer to the village. Makoto pointed out a familiar brick building. When they passed by, they winced at the bloody bones and scraps of clothing scattered about the street. Cody prayed quietly to himself. They walked further, and a scream cut through the pounding rain. There was no one on the road. No faces peering out from behind broken windows. Rue noticed movement barely visible in the downpour and saw Lyssa staggering between buildings. She shouted her name, but there was no answer. She chased after her through the dark alley.

Rue could see the village square at the other end. Somewhere close, the hounds began to howl and bark. A two-story building stood beside the alley. It was marred and damaged by fire. An exposed staircase led to the second floor, which was missing an exterior wall. The opening overlooked a courtyard. Lyssa scrambled up the stairs, and Rue followed closely behind her.

Lyssa stopped and stood there with her back to the doorway. "Lyssa?" Rue called to her gently. "It's me." Lyssa gasped and spun around, startled by her voice. Makoto and Cody gathered with Rue and saw that Lyssa still held a knife in her hand. She raised it to defend herself, and Rue could see the confusion in her eyes. The emptiness. Tears ran down Lyssa's face. They were those of a girl who was broken and alone and deeply afraid.

Rue slowly stepped forward. "Stay away from me!" Lyssa screeched.

"Lyssa, I need you to listen to me—okay?" said Rue. "None of us want to hurt you. We're your friends, and we love you."

"I don't know you!" Lyssa replied tearfully. "I don't even know where I am."

"You do know me, but you're upset right now. You've forgotten some things." Rue took another step toward her. Lyssa flinched and steadied her knife. "Lyssa, we found your diary. We know what you've been through—how much you've lost. I lost someone too, did you know that? I had a daughter once. Her name was Annete. But she was taken from me—just like your husband, Garrett."

Lyssa stood her ground, yet she trembled and mewled. "Garrett," she said softly through her strained voice. The knife began to wobble in her shaking hand.

Rue stepped forward one last time. "We tried to run from our problems back home. We gave up on ourselves. But it's time to accept our truths and help each other—so we can each have a second chance at a better life. So we can find peace. All you need to know right now is that you're loved. You don't have to be alone anymore."

Rue watched the expression on Lyssa's face change. It turned from fear and confusion to remembrance and understanding. A faint hope began to stir in her eyes, and the knife dropped to the ground. Rue reached out to embrace her as she approached. A loud bang rang out, and blood sprayed across Rue's body. Smoke filled the cold air. Lyssa looked down and saw she had been shot. Rue screamed at the sight of the exit wound in Lyssa's stomach. Cody winced, feeling a twinge of pain. He slid half of his jacket over and found he was bleeding too. The round had passed through Lyssa and grazed Rue, striking him in the side.

Lyssa stumbled and fell from the ledge onto the cobblestone below. Dolion crept out of hiding from behind where she had stood. There was a sheepish look on his face, and he was holding the pistol Makoto threw away. Rue snatched the gun from his quivering hand and put it to his head. She pulled the trigger six times. Six times, it clicked but never fired. There had been only one bullet left in the revolver, and he used it. She tossed the empty gun at him and rushed to Lyssa's side.

Cody touched his wound, and blood seeped through his shirt. He showed Dolion his bloody hand. "This you savin people again?" he asked.

"I didn't mean for it to hit you!" Dolion replied. "She would've killed one of you if I hadn't shot her!"

"Rue got through to her. We all know it."

"Don't you see? She's insane! She's possess—"

"Shut your fuckin mouth!" Cody yelled. He spat blood onto the ground and wiped his face with his sleeve. "Just shut up, for your own sake if not for mine. You say that cause it's what you want to believe, not cause it's true. You're exactly what's wrong with the world—with religion. You see evil or wrongdoin in everyone and everythin but yourself. And it's costin people their lives. What's it goin to cost you?"

Makoto saw Cody growing weaker and took his arm to support him. They made their way down the stairs, and Dolion sulked behind them. Rue was kneeling beside Lyssa, who lay on her back in the square. She lifted Lyssa's head to keep the rain from entering her nostrils, and blood ran down her face. She coughed, and it spurted from her mouth onto her dress. Rue held her in her arms and cried. "I'm sorry, little doe," Lyssa said.

"There's nothing to be sorry about."

"You didn't have to be my friend."

"You didn't have to be mine either, not after all you've been through."

"I'm sorry about your daughter."

"Me too."

"You should get out of here while you still—"

Lyssa's eyes shifted toward the others. A wild rage ignited inside her when she saw that Dolion was there. Her face contorted in anger. "You did this to me?" she asked as she spat up blood again. Dolion looked away. Lyssa tried to sit up but collapsed backward. The pain was too much for her to bear.

The survivors felt a menacing presence emerge in the village square. A cackle echoed against the cobblestone. The black cat. Gleeful, smiling. All the creatures that roamed the isle crept inward from the darkness surrounding them. The shapes with their white eyes. The feral hounds gnashing their teeth. The ravens gathered along the rooftops and amid the dead trees. The skull-faced monsters that ruled over them. Behind the horde lurked a horrific beast. The clouds broke for only a moment, and the moon cast a dim light upon the face of a hulking arachnid. Its orb-like eyes were almost invisible in the dark, like black planets clustered at the edge of space.

The throng of foul apparitions and cruel monsters erupted with sinister howling. They gleefully chortled and snarled. It terrified Rue and reminded her how hyenas circle their prey before devouring it alive. The elk-skull creature glided toward Lyssa, who, despite her surroundings, still glared at Dolion with hate in her eyes. Rue leaped to her feet. The monster approached Lyssa and placed its rawboned hand over her head. It whispered something to her. Something only she could understand. She whispered back, and Rue feared a deal was being made.

The creature released its grip on Lyssa's head. She screamed as her chest lurched into the air. Her body levitated, and she writhed in agony until the sound of her anguish turned to deranged laughter. Her pupils expanded like stellar voids, consuming all color until the eyes were of an opaque vacuity. The ravens swirled above like a brewing storm. Some landed atop her shoulders and some upon her outstretched arms.

The vile monsters continued to close in on the survivors. Their cacophony of sneering and hollering only grew in malice. Dolion panicked. He tried to run, but some unseen force dragged him to Lyssa. His knees buckled beneath him. He was compelled unwillingly to kneel before her. She lowered herself back to the ground, and he stared in terror.

The skull-faced creatures glided toward the remaining survivors, and it was then that Riel emerged. He stepped out from the alley and stood between them. The creatures hissed and spat at him. "Uriel, brother!" he shouted. "Cast down thy sword by which I might slay any who comes forth in wickedness."

"Who's Uriel?" whispered Rue. "And why is Riel talking like that?"

Makoto shook his head, but a look of fascination came over Cody's face. "Uriel is the angel they say guarded the entrance to the Garden of Eden with a fiery sword," he replied. "My God—Riel ain't some mystic like the professor thought. He's Gabriel, the archangel. Gabriel, the messenger."

"You mean an angel's been talking to me the whole time? Why didn't he tell us sooner?"

"I reckon some things aren't meant for us to know until they are."

Thunder boomed and shook the isle. Gabriel looked to the sky as an orange glow grew behind the gray clouds. There was a rhythmic whistling as it broke through the cover. Like a meteor falling to the earth, a spinning sword hurled downward and struck the ground at his feet. The blade was illuminated. Red hot, shedding embers into the air. Gabriel grabbed the handle, and flames ignited from the blade's edge. He wielded the weapon combatively and shouted, "You shall harm these people no further!"

"Wait, what about me?" asked Dolion.

Gabriel shook his head. "I am only here to defend those who have fulfilled the duties placed upon them." He then turned to Lyssa. "There was so much beauty in your soul. But the rage in your heart made you join a verboten evil. By your own choice, you will remain here. I am sorry."

Lyssa nodded acceptingly, but Dolion protested. "I'm a Christian, dammit! You have to save me!" he shouted.

"God will decide the fate of your soul. In the meantime, however, your physical self will stay here until you have given your last breath. You have only spread hate and despair and led people astray. And for that reason, I am not here to protect you."

Lyssa grinned and placed a finger under Dolion's chin, lifting his head. She looked into his eyes and caressed the side of his face in her hand. She ran her thumb over his cheek. "You're just a false prophet, aren't you?" she asked. "A wolf in sheep's clothing."

"N-no," he said, shuttering.

"Pathetic that after all this, you still haven't learned a fucking thing."

"Please, don't kill me. I'm begging you."

"Don't worry. I'll give you a good death. You've earned it."

Dolion tried to pull away, but it was no use.

"No, wai—"

Lyssa grabbed Dolion's head in both her hands. He pulled at her arms as she held him in place. She was too strong. She smiled as the ravens dove at him with an unnatural fury. They pecked at his face and took his eyes with them. Rue and the others watched in horror as Dolion screamed in pain. When the ravens ceased their attack, he stood there shaking and whimpering and blind. He stumbled about and tried to find safety but knew not which direction to go.

Lyssa twitched her head back and forth in subtle jerks, directing the ravens like a conductor leading an orchestra. They nipped at Dolion from each side, guiding his steps as he drifted from right to left. The beasts and apparitions snickered and snarled and cleared a path for him, save for all but one creature that did not move. Blind and unaware, he approached it. The arachnid did not hesitate. It snatched him up and carried him off into the darkness. The off-rhythm taps of its rapid, scurried steps faded as it retreated to its nest.

"Rue," Gabriel said softly, "go where we first met. There is a door inside you previously found locked. You now have the key. Go there, and you will find your way home."

Rue checked her pockets and found a key that was not there before. She looked at Cody and Makoto.

Cody looked ill. His clothes were soaked in blood. They helped him stay on his feet as they left the village square. When Rue looked back, she saw the creatures had departed and Lyssa with them. Tears ran down Rue's face. She mourned her friend. She had seen her climb back from the edge of insanity only for one man to push her over it, and the rage that grew like cancer inside her consumed her entirely. A demon's offer to let Lyssa unleash her violence and avenge herself for all she endured was more than she could resist. She chose not only to accept death but to embrace it.

Truth

Rue and Makoto helped Cody to the church. The rain had stopped, and the moon shone at its brightest. The isle was quiet. As calm as the day Rue arrived. They pushed open the doors and went inside. They passed one of the upright pews, and Cody halted and gestured toward it. "Please," he said, "I need to sit."

"But we're almost there," urged Rue.

"I need to sit."

Cody slumped onto the pew. He leaned back and painfully let out a groan. "Y'all go ahead," he said. "I'll be right behind you."

"You can barely stand on your own," Makoto replied.

"I'll be alright."

"We need to get you help," Rue said insistently.

"It's fine. Just go ahead."

Makoto paused and studied his face. "You're not coming," he said.

Cody shook his head. "I ain't makin it," he replied. "Lost too much blood—I can feel it. There ain't no way I'm gettin to a hospital in time to make a difference. Seein as where I been shot, I ain't sure I was ever goin to make it."

"We can't just leave you here," replied Rue.

"It's okay, darlin. I done what I was brought here to do. I'm an old man. I've lived my life. At least if I die here, I die sober, helpin my friends. I just wish I could've helped more. Especially Lyssa. My heart hurts for her. She might've chose to be one of them things, but she didn't deserve it.

"I spent a long time thinkin I'd given up on religion. But what I see now is that it was never God I was mad at. It was church folk. Maybe not all of em, but the kind that pretend to be acceptin and well-intentioned yet are no different than those who forced that girl into existence just to chase her into the flames. Without even the slightest feeling of responsibility or compassion, they look the other way. Excuse it, no doubt, in the name of some verse they redefine to justify their actions—just like Dolion. They can see the results of what they done play out in front of their eyes, but it still don't matter to em. In their minds, there ain't no provin em wrong. They'd do it again without a second thought.

"Lyssa suffered her whole life, and every time a believer had an opportunity to help her, they made things worse. Not one of em ever batted an eye at the last one, neither. No accountability cause they don't like talkin about their own if it makes em all look bad. Frankly, it don't seem like they evolved much beyond the mentality they had when killin people for believin em to be witches—they just found quieter, more civil ways of carryin on their prejudice. Ways that make it easier to pass the blame so they can sleep at night.

"Me? I've never felt closer to God than when I'm just bein kind to people without expecting anything in return. Not their salvation or adherence to a book I only pretend to understand. Cause it ain't all about me and what I believe. It's between them and God, and my faith is between me and God, and boy, do me and God got a lot to talk about. I got so many questions."

"That's the truth," Rue said.

Cody grinned slightly. "Truth. We've used that word often since we met, haven't we?"

Rue nodded. "A few times."

"If there's one truth above all to take away from this place, it's that everyone's got em. Hidden and locked away. Put out of sight and out of mind. But the truths we don't face are scarier than any monsters we think up or ghosts that might haunt us. They're what separate us from good and evil. Life and death. Humility and self-righteousness. Belief in 'the' God or all gods or absolute nihilism. They determine how we get up and face our lives and the kind of people we're goin to be today, tomorrow, and evermore. But if we're willin to take a hard look at ourselves, there's always a chance to change our stories. Maybe even make a difference in someone else's."

Rue leaned over and hugged Cody tightly. "I'm going to miss you," she said.

"Me too, darlin," he replied, "and you too, Koto."

Makoto nodded solemnly and gripped Cody's shoulder. "Do you want us to stay with you until—"

"No need. I won't be alone."

"What do you mean?" Rue asked.

"Gabriel sent somebody to fetch me," he said. "The more I feel myself fade, the clearer I can see her."

"See who?"

"Faina. She's come to take me away from this place. Y'all better leave too. Don't worry about me. Just be good so I can see y'all again someday, okay?"

"Okay."

"Oh, and Rue?"

"Yeah?"

"You keep prayin for that girl. You never know."

Rue nodded. She withdrew from Cody as tears filled her eyes. She walked with Makoto to the back rooms, and stood before the locked door. She reached into her pocket for the key and looked up at Makoto. A tear ran down his cheek. "Are you alright?" she asked.

"Yeah," he said. "Just promise me one thing."

"What's that?"

"Whatever is behind this door, and no matter where it takes us, we won't forget each other."

Rue hugged Makoto and smiled softly. "Never."

She inserted the ornate skeleton key into the lock and turned it until she felt it click into place. The door opened into an empty room, far larger than possible inside the small church. They wondered if it was real. In the center of the floor was a black, cavernous hole, like a deep well in which no end could be seen. Rue and Makoto stared into its infinite darkness. They looked at each other one last time. They stepped forward, hand in hand, and dropped into the void beneath them. All concepts of time and space were lost, and their consciousness faded too.

Ravens

Rue jolted awake to a ship horn blowing off the coast. She sat up and found herself inside a vessel wedged into a sandy, wet shoreline. Sunlight beamed from the sky above. Its radiant warmth washed over her, and she saw her wounds were gone. She heard the calls of seagulls and the rolling of cars on a nearby road. Rue walked up the beach and saw a fisherman heading the other way. She asked what day it was and thought she had misheard the answer. *No, that must be wrong,* she thought. *It can't be.*

Rue continued until she reached a road. On the sidewalk, a man sold magazines and newspapers from a stand. She checked for the date in a newspaper. "Is this today?" she asked.

"Nah, I only sell old news," he said sarcastically. "Of course it's today." Rue felt hope come over her and rushed home as fast as she could. When she reached her house, she anxiously stood outside. Her blood ran cold at the thought of what she knew had happened there. She wondered if it could all be different.

The sound of a vehicle drew close from up the road. A moment later, a bright yellow school bus stopped there in the street. Several children departed and went into neighboring homes, and the bus began to drive away. Rue's heart sank. It casually passed by her. Then it slammed on its brakes, and its doors slid open. A little girl stepped off the bus, and Rue dropped to her knees. Annete ran to her and hugged her tightly. *Sorry, Mommy,* she signed. *I almost missed my stop. I didn't know the driver called my name.*

That's okay, hon. You're here now.

How come you're not at work?

They said I could go home.

Does this mean you're making dinner tonight?

How about we go out to eat?

Can we please?

Of course, but I was hoping you could do something

for me when we get inside.
What do you want me to do?
Help me pack your favorite things.

Rue watched over Annete, who slept beside her. She brushed the hair from her small face and looked through the airplane window at the vast ocean below. There was an island, and though it was not where she had endured so much, she thought of her friends. She said a silent prayer and held in her hand the bracelet Lyssa had made her.

Rue arrived in the city with her daughter. She fetched a cab, which took them to a busy street. It was filled with shops and vendors. Rue stepped out of the vehicle and took her daughter's hand and looked up. They gazed in awe at the vibrant neon signs that decorated the tall buildings towering over them. There were people all around. Some were on foot, and some on bicycles. She could not understand them. She did not speak their language.

Rue pulled a wrinkled paper from her pocket and glanced down at it. On the paper was an image with an address she had written down. She looked up from it and scanned the street with her eyes, comparing each store to the one in her picture. In a small shop across from her, there stood a clerk sweeping the floor. He looked up at Rue, and they locked eyes. Makoto smiled.

Somewhere out there in the unknown, a man wakes atop a low dune. The sky is a terrible gray. Detritus is strewn across the beach. Strips of seaweed are tangled within the laces of his wet boots. He takes them off and cleans them and puts them back on again. He looks out over the horizon, but no ship is in sight.

The man notices the wood line behind him. Something gracefully moves between the trees. He narrows his eyes to focus them and sees the faint outline of a woman. As she walks, ravens follow.

A moment later, she is gone. The man heads toward the forest, unsure what he might find upon the pale isle of gloam.

About the author

Mark Gulino is a fiction and non-fiction writer. He has worked as a top-rated *Upwork* freelancer and as an editor for the *Forbes*-featured online publication *Gadget Flow*. He also created and wrote the award-nominated science fiction podcast, *A Journey Beyond the Skies,* for which he won "Best Storyteller in a Storytelling Production (2020)." *Upon the Pale Isle of Gloam* is Mark's first book.

Author Photo © 2023 by Mark Gulino

Thank you for reading my debut novella. I hope you enjoyed reading it as much as I enjoyed writing it. I'm excited to begin working on my next project, but in the meantime, please be sure to follow me on social media. You can find links at www.markgulino.com.

—See you there.

Content Warning

This book describes scenes of intense violence and includes references to abuse and sexual assault. Strong language is used throughout. There are mentions of animal cruelty, suicide, alcoholism, and the use of drugs and alcohol. It also contains dark subject content and religious themes. Please read with care.

If you or someone you know is struggling or in a crisis, help is available at www.samhsa.gov. You can also call or text 988 to reach the suicide and crisis hotline.

www.ingramcontent.com/pod-product-compliance
Lightning Source LLC
Chambersburg PA
CBHW031949170626
46807CB00006B/2411